In the glow of the red light, Trace saw that the boy's dark eyes were shiny with tears. But, as the doors closed, what he also saw . . . what he could *not* have really seen . . . were the books on the shelf behind the boy. The little boy was looking right at him. And Trace could see right through him.

# Trace

## Pat Cummings

**HARPER**

*An Imprint of HarperCollinsPublishers*

Library of Congress Control Number: 2018034250

ISBN 978-0-06-269885-8

Typography by David Curtis

20 21 22 23 24   PC/BRR   10 9 8 7 6 5 4 3 2

❖

First paperback edition, 2020

To Art Cummings and Jackie Carter

# *Trace's Family Tree*

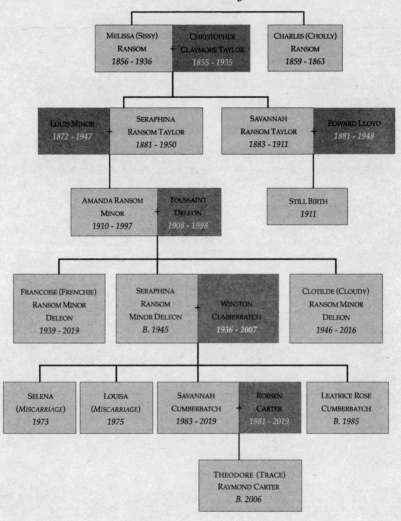

*Car door!*

Green water was rising, crawling, clawing up his legs. Not again. And that smell. Too green, too deep, too *river*. Long-fingered water pulled at his knees, inching up now, almost gingerly tugging at his waist. The car door wouldn't open! What? Was Mom talking to him? Silence. But no, her lips were moving. Was she . . . *praying*? He didn't dare answer, could not chance opening his mouth. Warm water was lapping at his chin, softly, greedily. And her eyes. He felt sick for her. Water was filling her eyes. Turning them that same awful green. *Car door!* And Dad. Just banging, banging, banging the stupid windows, kicking glass that wouldn't break. Too late now, those dark hands had found him, *again*, pulled at his slippery arms, *again*. No! *Missed her!* Clammy green fingers were slipping along the edges of his lips now, trying to tease them open. *Car door!*

It. Wouldn't. Open! Water flooded into his mouth. *Missed her! Car door!*

"Mr. Carter!"

"*Uuhhh?*" Trace jerked awake and away from the sharp punch in his back. He struggled to place himself. Class. Mrs. Weaver, hand on one hip, loomed over his desk, waiting for an answer to *something*. Scattered giggling surrounded him and someone near the door snorted.

"Sorry, I, uh . . ." Trace wiped a trail of drool from the corner of his mouth. Behind him there was a burst of coughing followed by unintelligible sputtering. The punch had definitely awakened him, but even if his friend Ty, in the seat behind him, had hacked up a lung trying to warn him, he still had no idea what Mrs. Weaver wanted.

Six of his classmates stood in front of the chalk-board, looking bored and annoyed. Waiting. For him. Trace blinked at the board, hoping for a clue. But the string of dates written on it told him nothing: 1800, 1810, 1820, 1830, 1840, 1850. Each year had a name under it and each of the students held a piece of yellow chalk.

"Sometime today, Mr. Carter," Mrs. Weaver said wearily. She handed him a stump of yellow chalk. The room felt too warm. A hiss of steam escaped from the radiators. Tree branches slapped across the windows, shaking off leaves that flattened themselves against the glass, desperate not to fall. The clock on the wall clunked softly, its second hand flinching as another minute died.

Trace's friend Tiberius, the only one in class who might *not* be enjoying his embarrassment, gave him another punch from behind, gentler this time.

Trace took the chalk reluctantly and joined his classmates at the board, ignoring their scowls. Mrs. Weaver peered over her glasses at the rest of the class and called out, "Ms. Stringer!"

Yolanda Stringer was unfortunately named. Long and gangly, with dishwater-blond hair masking her eyes, she fit her Stringbean nickname. Trace had never called her that though. Hunching out from her desk, she slumped forward, accepted a piece of chalk, scrawled

*1870* on the board, and signed her name below that.

"Put your year up, wacko," she whispered loudly to Trace.

"Need help counting, freak boy?" Lou Pagano hissed from his other side.

Trace turned, ignoring them, tuning them out. He sized up the sequence of numbers and wrote *1860* and his name on the board. This had to be the timeline project they had talked about last Friday. But Stringbean had called *him* wacko? And Lou the Schnozz thought *he* was the freak? Losers. With his back to the room, Trace closed his eyes momentarily. This did not count. This was not his class. These were not his friends. He breathed slowly and turned around. Sticks and stones.

His head felt soggy. Licking his dry, cracked lips only made them sticky. And it seemed there was something else . . . something gritty. Like mud. River-bottom mud. He still smelled it. It was always going to be there, wasn't it? Trace looked at Mrs. Weaver, willing her, *begging* her, commanding her, to let them go. He wanted to sit down now, maybe put his head between his knees, or open a window and breathe in as much air as his lungs could hold. But the small,

4

round woman was busily recording what was written on the board.

"Okay. You eight will pick in, um, hold on . . ." Mrs. Weaver scrawled their names on eight index cards, folded them quickly, and dropped them into the Elvis vase she kept on her desk. Grabbing the ceramic head, she shook it violently, then plunged a chubby hand into what would have been the King's frontal lobe.

". . . in this order: Theodore first, Damon, Kristin, Winston, Haeyoun, Yolanda, Louis, then Marcus."

The unusual pleasure of being called first for anything, for winning something even remotely like a contest, was quickly replaced by confusion. Pick what? Trace scanned the room.

Kali Castleberry had her head down, scribbling in her notebook, ignoring him as always. It was the top of her head, the way the rows of perfectly woven braids did not allow a single stray hair to escape even now at the end of the day, that let him know: he was supposed to be picking study partners and he had better not pick her.

"Today, Mr. Carter," Mrs. Weaver groaned. "Please choose two people, TODAY." The teacher had squeezed her wide hips into the swivel chair behind her desk, a chair that had long ago surrendered under the weight of her failed diets. Listing to one side, it creaked in pain as, with a weary sigh, the teacher leveled her eyes upon him and rested her chins atop the vase. Elvis gave him a sideways grin. *Go for it, man.*

All in all, it had not been a horrible day. Tiberius was running late, so Trace ran into the deli next to the Bergen Street station. Grabbing a bottle of juice, he got on line behind three girls he recognized from his biology class. They were talking loudly and nonstop. But although he saw them twice a week, they made it clear when he smiled at them that they were not talking to him. Trace glanced out the deli window. What was taking Ty so long?

He was studying the faces of kids as they streamed down the sidewalk toward the subway entrance when he noticed a small boy. The kid was too little to be alone on the street, but no one seemed to be with him. His hair was a mess, his clothes were disheveled. Even from across the street, that much was clear. Trace looked down briefly to dig two dollars out of his pants pocket for the juice. When he looked again, the boy was staring right at him. A shiver raced through his chest. But why would he . . . what was the . . . ?

"You just gonna show me the juice, or are you buyin' it, kid?" The man behind the register was glaring at him, one eyebrow raised. The girls had gone. Trace paid for the juice, then turned back to the window, almost afraid to see the kid again. But all he saw was Tiberius hurrying past the window and descending into the subway.

"Hey, Ty, wait up!" Trace called. By the time he caught up with his friend on the platform, he was out of breath and the kid was forgotten. "What's happening, man? You ran right past me."

"Oh. Did I *overlook* you?" Tiberius huffed.

"Wha . . . ?" Trace shook his head as though he was shaking out loose parts. "What's eating *you*?"

Tiberius glared at him, then turned to face the empty tunnel, as if their train was approaching. He said nothing for minutes, leaving Trace to stare at his friend's back. A faint olive image of SpongeBob that had been inked over with a marker grinned weakly from Ty's backpack. Trace shook his head.

"A girl?" Tiberius finally snarled. "You picked a girl first and just left me hanging out there?"

Trace had to stop himself from laughing. Ty

couldn't be serious. When would he have ever gotten to have the first pick like that again? So, yeah. He could choose Kali Castleberry, unattainable goddess and überpopular school beauty who was unaware of his existence (and who would surely have been scooped up when demon Damon made the second pick), or he could choose his best and, admittedly, only friend, Tiberius. He should not have to explain this.

"You're kidding, right?" Trace asked. "C'mon, man. When would I get a crack at ever even talking to her again? You knew I was gonna call you next. I had to take my shot."

No one would have chosen Tiberius first. Trace knew it. He suspected Ty knew it. Tiberius was a classic leftover, just like Trace would have been if he hadn't been the one doing the choosing. A chubby Chinese American graffiti artist slash would-be rapper and a scrawny black new kid whose weekly therapy sessions seemed to be common knowledge just weren't going to top any popularity list. Not at Intermediate School 99 in the People's Republic of Brooklyn. Not on Planet Earth.

He nudged his friend. "Hey, I had to go for it, Ty."

A warm rush of sweaty air announced the arrival of their train. It would have been easy to get separated in the brusque exchange of bodies getting on and off as the doors dinged open. But Ty moved slowly, letting Trace keep up with him. The apology had been accepted.

Leatrice Anne Cumberbatch, long-limbed and cinnamon-colored like Trace's mom, was staring into a steaming pot on the stove when Trace arrived. Home. This was not home. Every time he slid his key into the scarred lock on the weathered door of the ramshackle brownstone at this bedraggled end of Vanderbilt Avenue, Trace reminded himself: this is not home.

"Hey, hey, hey, mister," Auntie Lea sang out. "You are in for a treat tonight." His aunt had headphones on, and whatever she was listening to was so loud that Trace could make out the wail of a saxophone from where he stood in the doorway to the kitchen. She didn't wait for a response, just danced from sink to stove to refrigerator, bobbing her head. The kitchen table, a huge plank of raw wood that had been painted a deep forest green, was piled with colorful hemp bags of fresh vegetables. The smells emanating from the stove gave nothing away.

Trace took the stairs two at a time, shrugging off his backpack when he reached his room on the second floor. Technically, it was not his room. Know *that*, he said quietly to himself. He kicked off his sneakers and climbed a short ladder to the loft bed where he slept. The room had a split personality: half his, half his aunt's studio. But it was all hers really. The bed and the little work space right underneath it held practically everything he owned. A photographer's lamp, clamped to the underside of the ladder, illuminated his small desk. Its drawers were crammed with worn sketchbooks, the few CDs he had, letters, paper, batteries, chewed pens, yearbooks from his school in Baltimore, his mom's snow globe, his dad's cuff links, a deck of cards from Disney World. Junk.

Auntie Lea had cleared the walls in the room, offering them up as his to claim. They were still blank. Before he had arrived, the room had been her studio. In front of two tall windows that overlooked a small patch of grass sat her handmade table, half covered with trays of beads. She must have cleaned out a Box Bag n' Bin store, because her many pairs of pliers, tiny screwdrivers, spools of clear and black nylon thread, and tubes of shiny sequins all lived in their own little compartments, arm's length from her work stool. Auntie Lea made jewelry. She did not seem to make *money* from her jewelry, but that didn't matter to her. It was, she had told Trace repeatedly, her "passion."

Auntie Lea had a lot of passions.

Music. Dance. Photography. Cooking. He had known about her many interests from family visits, back when he was too little to be wary of her experiments in the kitchen. Knitting. Conceptual art. Astrology. Numerology. Many of Auntie Lea's passions ended in *-ology*. "She's been talking with aliens again," his dad would say, winking as he handed over the phone for Trace to say hello whenever they called her.

When Trace had come to live with her in August, his aunt had tried to get him to talk about what his "passion" might be. But that was after the accident. After everything had frozen and he found he did not have to answer questions, could not have answered if he had wanted to. Trace knew his aunt meant well.

But if he looked at her too long he saw his mom's eyes, his mom's elegant jawline and the high cheekbones he knew he himself had inherited. And those few times when she forgot and touched his arm or tried to hug him, he felt as though a wave was sweeping into him, surprising him with a sudden, unpleasant sensation of being off-balance.

Auntie Lea was his mother's baby sister, so he loved her like you love an aunt you only see on holidays. Like an aunt who had time to listen to you babble when you were too little for words but fascinated by phones. She was the spacey aunt who kept an eye out for UFOs, chatted with houseplants, and saw signs everywhere in everything. If the universe was sending messages, his aunt was all ears. But what good were signs that didn't come in time? That weren't clear? Auntie Lea was cool. But, no. Trace didn't have a passion to offer up when she asked. What he had was a blank.

Kicking off his sneakers, he stretched his legs to rest his feet on the ceiling. This was his thinking position. A burst of laughter came from downstairs, followed by singing. It was not his aunt's voice. The doorbell rang. "Grand Central Station." He sighed. An endless stream of what his mom would call the "fringe element" always turned up at mealtimes on Vander-bilt. The right thing to do would be to go downstairs and offer to help. His aunt would be thrilled. Trace walked his feet along the ceiling and looked around the room.

In Baltimore, his bedroom walls had been plas-tered with pictures of athletes and singers, calendars, schedules, and photos of friends and family. Here, a box stuffed with photographs sat on a shelf in his closet, right next to the bed. That first night in this apartment, after the funeral, after days of lawyers and city offices and scores of gray people, Auntie Lea had held out the box to him as though it were a sacred treasure. But Trace had not taken it, touched it, or even watched as she set it on the closet shelf.

"Whenever you want it, Theo," she had whispered. His aunt had draped an arm around his shoulders, squeezing them gently, and kissed his forehead. He had had to hold on to the ladder, waiting for the wave to pass until she let go and tiptoed to the door. But why be so quiet? Why tiptoe when stomping and shouting made more sense?

"I know it won't be easy," Auntie Lea said. "I miss them too, so very, very much." She had waited. But

Trace had nothing to say. "This is your home now," she added softly. And that had been that.

Trace let his long legs fall back to the bed. He could not look at their pictures. He could not even open the box. Nothing could go on those walls. Because everything he hung up, *anything* he hung up, would be instead of them, covering them or trying to get past them.

"Theo!" his aunt called. "Dinner!"

For a minute, Trace felt a spark of hope as he reached the kitchen. There was a sweet, tangy smell of barbecue in the air. Brenda, his aunt's friend, and Dawoud, her partner, were already at the table, their plates loaded. Trace loved barbecued anything. He detoured quickly to wash his hands before Auntie Lea had to remind him.

"Theodore Raymundo Carter, my man!" Dawoud said as Trace slid into his seat. Since arriving in Brooklyn, Theodore Raymond Carter had heard enough variations on his name to make him immune to any teasing.

On day one at IS 99, his chem lab partner had been Tiberius Q. Lee. Until he met Ty, Trace had gone all day without speaking to another student. In every class, the teachers had made a point of reading his name and introducing him as "new." Without fail, the name Theodore was met with winces, rolled eyes, and scattered snickers. By lunchtime, he had heard *The Odor*, *Thermador*, and *The Ogre* as he passed students in the halls. The names were never launched directly at him—they were just laughing whispers that sailed by as he searched for his next class.

At lunchtime, the cafeteria had been a canyon of noise. The constant buzz of laughing, flirting, and fussing that dominated the big room made Trace think of a hive. All these bees knew one another, they shared stories and secrets, and they probably knew one another's families. So he had gone to the far wall to a table where only a few places were taken, a table clearly designated for outcasts. No one spoke to him, and by the time fifth period arrived, he just wanted the day to end.

"This is Theotus Carter, class," Mr. Domenici, the chemistry teacher, said drily. Trace considered correcting him. But why bother? No one had looked up. Three rows of lab tables held beakers, microscopes, and matching sets of shiny instruments. A bank of computers ran along the rear wall. Mr. Domenici scratched at the stubble on his chin and motioned toward a seat near the window. "You can partner with Ty for today," the teacher decided.

Tiberius Q. Lee was the only one in the class without a partner. The dark-haired boy introduced himself with his full name and began arranging petri dishes on their table.

"What does the *Q* stand for?" Trace had asked.

"*See you*," Tiberius answered.

"Uh, sure," Trace said. "But what's the *Q* stand for?"

Tiberius had turned to study him. "Qiu. Q—I-U," he said evenly. "It's pronounced sort of like '*see you*.' It was my mom's last name and it means *autumn* in Mandarin. Since I was born in October, they thought it made double sense. The 'Tiberius' I owe to Captain James T. Kirk. Dad's a hard-core Trekkie." Tiberius had paused, his chin slightly raised, as though bracing for a wisecrack. But Trace said nothing, so he simply nodded. "Just call me Ty."

"Theodore Raymond Carter," Trace had said.

Ty shook his head. "Won't work," he said. "They'll eat you alive with that one."

Mr. Domenici was handing out worksheets and the

room fell silent as the teacher cheerfully described the collection of horrifying germs that might be identified on the samples they had been given. The contents of the little dishes on Trace's table looked innocent enough: one held a penny, one had a smear of what looked like dried mustard; there was a pink eraser in one and a rubber band in another.

By the time he and Ty had figured out that they were risking their lives by handling the samples, he had decided to rename himself Trace. T. Ray C. He had considered Tracy, but that could be a girl's name. He needed something sharp-edged and mysterious. Something that, if they had to whisper it in the halls at him, would sound cool. Trace.

He had finished his dinner quickly. No amount of barbecue sauce could turn tofu into chicken, but his aunt's rice was delicious. Yes, there were strange, crunchy little green things in it, but, having eaten one accidentally and liked the taste, he decided to embrace the mystery. Auntie Lea ate no meat, no eggs, and no vowel vegetables. Asparagus, eggplant, onions, okra . . . Trace was no fan of them either. Certain random vegetables that began with a consonant were on his aunt's list as honorary vowels: squash, brussels sprouts, cabbage. Trace had no one to invite to dinner, so there was really no need to decode her system. This was one of his aunt's quirks that would never embarrass him.

Auntie Lea did not own a cookbook. She got an idea, invited one or more of her QTs, as she called them, or "Cuties," and dinner was served. The Queen's Tasters. Kings had official tasters, his aunt said. Their job was to taste whatever the king was to be served in case it had been poisoned by an enemy. If the taster didn't drop dead, the king knew the food was fine. In the short time that Trace had lived there, he had gotten in the habit of waiting for the Cuties to be served first at dinner. *Such a polite young man*, they would say, misunderstanding his motive. If no one keeled over dead, Trace would fix himself a plate.

Most of the Cuties were artists of one kind or another. Auntie Lea occasionally worked as a freelance production assistant, setting up photo shoots for magazines, music labels, and theater productions. In the two months that Trace had lived there, she had made at least a dozen new friends on various shoots, not a one of them who seemed to have a real job.

"I hope youse guys saved room for dessert," she cracked, turning on her Brooklynese. "I call this Coney Island custard."

Dawoud beamed. Brenda hurriedly cleared away plates to make room for the quivering mound of shiny yellow pudding that Auntie Lea brought to the table. It did sort of remind Trace of a roller coaster at Coney Island. There were definitely peaks and valleys. Bits of strawberries and blueberries, embedded in the slick, molded dessert, circled their way to the top, where a layer of dried apricots, nuts, and raisins swayed and cracked as the dessert came to rest on the table. It was scary.

"You've outdone yourself, Lea!" Dawoud exclaimed.

"May I?" said Brenda, bravely scooping spoonfuls into bowls for everyone.

Auntie Lea had only moved to Brooklyn earlier that year herself, but she seemed to make new friends every time she left the house. The Korean grocer on Myrtle Avenue told her jokes. The Indian man at the corner newsstand debated politics with her. Even the Italian barista working the counter at Starbucks ignored the line when she arrived to give her updates on which beans had the most subtle or nutty or *robusto* flavor.

In two months, the only person Trace knew was Tiberius. And that was because Mr. Domenici had put them together.

The shivering, gelatinous pudding slumped before him, looking wounded after Brenda's assault. Trace excused himself. He was full. He was suddenly sleepy. He had massive amounts of homework to do. He had a headache. He could not remember how many excuses he unspooled as he left the table. But he did know that he did not have a single friend, no one, who would taste Auntie Lea's Coney Island custard for *him*. And that sucked.

# 3

Trace had done enough research while he ate breakfast to feel armed with tidbits about the 1860s that might impress Kali if he ran into her before class. He was not sure if they were sticking to United States history or if they had to cover the whole world. But she would know. In class, she was the one who always had all the answers. He smiled just thinking about her. She was gorgeous *and* smart.

Trace sprinted across Bergen Street. The subway gods had been on his side today: he was early. With any luck, Kali would be lingering on the front steps with her girlfriends. He had struck gold with the 1860s: the Pony Express had just started, Jesse

James and his brother Frank were robbing banks like crazy, and Abraham Lincoln not only got elected president, but he'd gotten himself assassinated, all in *his* decade. Trace could not help but grin: this was good stuff.

He and Kali could chat about Jesse James. Maybe over lunch. There was that coffee shop on Smith Street that made those sandwich wraps that girls liked. Trace's smile widened. It had nice booths and cool music playing whenever he walked by. Maybe they could do research there after school. He made a note to himself to see if the place had Wi-Fi or not.

Kali and the girls she hung out with talked like they *loved* gangsters. He had overheard them in the cafeteria, in the hallway leaning against their lockers, in line at assemblies. He had even followed behind them once as they headed for the subway. The movies they talked about, the song lyrics they bounced off one another, even the way they snapped back at any stray guy who dared to approach without clearance convinced Trace that Jesse James would be his golden ticket with Kali. James was the original gangster, a serious OG. Skimming an online biography, Trace had lit on the word *bushwhacker*. He could read up on it later, but now, as he approached the school, he practiced letting it roll off his tongue.

"Yeah, that Jesse was a real *bushwhacker*, huh?"

"Did you check out that *bushwhacker* Jesse James yet?"

"Man, what a *bushwhacker* James turned out to be!"

Kali and her girls were lingering around the door just as he had hoped. He watched as Damon bounded up the steps and said something to them. Then he leaned in like he was going to kiss Dani Perez, a tiny, curly-haired girl who must have emptied the shelves at the Salvation Army for her outfit. Unfortunately for Damon, the look came with combat boots. One of them connected with Damon's shin just as Dani smacked him on the side of his head. The girl was quick.

Trace flinched as Damon recoiled in pain. That was *not* going to happen to him. Hesitating at the foot of the steps, he breathed in the crisp fall air and repeated the word to himself: *bushwhacker*. Feeling a surge of determination, he climbed the stairs in time to see Damon limping past the school guard in the lobby. He heard the girls laughing over Damon's takedown, but Trace stayed focused only on Kali, whose back was turned to him.

"H . . . h . . . hey, Kali!" he said. He had hoped to sound confident, but it had come out kind of like a bark. His voice sounded rough, as though it hadn't been used in a long time and had cracked in places. Kali slowly turned, but only her face, to look at him over her shoulder.

"Did you check out that gangster Jesse James yet?" Trace said brightly. Silence. Trace pressed on. "What a bushwhacker, huh?" He grinned, nodding, waiting for the light to go on in Kali's eyes. Around her, the faces of the other girls registered confusion, distaste, and annoyance. Dani sniffed as though she were picking up a whiff of something foul.

"Do I know you?" Kali said drily. Her eyes traveled down to his shoes. Trace looked down too, even though his brain was screaming at him to play it off. Silently, he cursed himself for wearing those beat-up sneakers with the ratty laces. He had new laces. He could see them still wrapped in plastic, spotless, sitting on the middle shelf of the cabinet in the bathroom. And he had been meaning to clean the grime off these sneakers. Not cool.

Trace cleared his throat. "We're in the same—" he

began. But Kali had turned away. She shook her head and one of her girls, tall, with bizarro eyeglasses and a face splotchy with freckles, signaled a V to him with her hand. "*Váyate*," she mouthed in case Trace had missed her point. Beat it.

*Seriously?*

At least it was Friday. Trace had dreaded this last class, but when it was over, the day would finally end. Nodding at Tiberius, he slid into his seat by the window just as the bell rang. Mrs. Weaver spent most of the class sneezing and coughing and blathering on about revolution and exploration and what an adventurous "thentury" the 1800s was. Her cheeks were flushed and her eyes were wet. She had to run out of steam soon, but Trace did not dare look at the clock.

He kept his eyes straight ahead. No way was he going to look at or near the door. No way would he glance at that entire side of the room where Kali sat. They would have to talk eventually, of course. She would have to work with him. But that was it. All business. No more Mr. Pleasant. Mr. Helpful. Mr. Do Some Research and Share It. No more Mr. Friendly.

"For the lath fifteen minutes of clath I want you to break into your sthudy groups," Mrs. Weaver sniffed.

Around her neck on a cord hung a half-used roll of toilet paper. Every few minutes, she unwound a foot or so of tissue from the roll and noisily blew her nose. "By next Friday, be prepared to give your prethentations." She snorted loudly and the gurgle of mucus being inhaled brought on a chorus of *eewww*s and *gross*es and *puh-leeeese*s from the girls in class.

Mrs. Weaver lowered her glasses to the tip of her reddened nose and scanned the room. "Thank you for your conthern," she said sarcastically. "Now, break into your groupths, and Prethley"—she turned and motioned to a girl who had been absent the day before—"you join Theo's group, pleeth." Waving her hands as though mixing a witch's brew, Mrs. Weaver oversaw the chair sliding and desk scraping that followed.

Trace did not move. If Mrs. Weaver herself tried to budge him, he would not take one step toward Kali. But he did not have to. Ty was scooting his desk around to face him just as Presley Jackson slid into a nearby seat that had been abandoned when everyone shifted places. In extreme slow motion and with an air of complete and utter weariness, Kali walked over and perched on the windowsill by the three of them. Sitting *with* them was clearly out of the question.

"Okay," Tiberius said, whipping out his iPhone and punching up Google. "Lincoln's elected, we've got the Civil War, oh, cool . . . the Battle of Bull Run. I want that." He pulled out a pad of paper and began making notes.

"Ooooh, can I do Lincoln's assassination?" Presley asked. "I love, love, *love* the theater. There was this musical I tried out for—"

"He got shot. He died. End of story," said Kali. Crossing her arms, she rolled her eyes heavenward, then breathed the word *pa-THET-ic* toward the ceiling. "We need to divvy this up fairly," she continued. "I'm not getting stuck with doing all the work while you guys pick out one no-brainer event to cover."

"Look," Trace said gruffly. "We're just discussing what went on in general, okay? We need to get an overview." Not only was Kali rude, she was what his mom called a *prima donna*. Now they glared at each other. This was not exactly what he had had in mind at breakfast when he had daydreamed about looking into her eyes. When he had hoped that working together might make her actually *see* him. She mouthed the word *overview* and shook her head as though Trace had been trying to impress her.

Fine. Let them slice up the decade without him. Trace sat back and studied the tree outside as Ty rattled off events, claiming most of the major Civil War battles for himself. Presley called dibs on Lincoln and practically every invention that Ty mentioned: the typewriter, motorcycles, advancements in photographic film. Kali took the Pony Express and Black Friday, a day when the gold market crashed and banks in New York apparently went ballistic.

"Oh, yeah," Kali added, leaning over to tap the pad where Tiberius was taking notes, "put me down to report on Jesse James, too." She smiled sweetly at Ty. "He was *such* a bushwhacker."

That did it. Trace felt his legs twitch. They were itching to get up, walk to the door, and go. They would carry him out of the building, across the Brooklyn Bridge, through the Holland Tunnel, and all the way down I-95 to Baltimore if he just stood up now and let them. Later for this.

Ty was watching him, a frown creasing his brow. "So, that leaves all the race stuff, Trace. You cool with that?" he asked.

Trace nodded and said nothing.

"Okay, man," Tiberius said. He ticked off topics as he made notes. "That means you've got the whole slavery thing, the Black Codes, the draft riots, the KKK . . ." Ty looked up from his list. "Maybe we can split things up after we start researching. This is a lot."

"Don't worry about it," Trace said in a low voice. He glanced at the clock. He could not hear it over the good-natured fussing and haggling rising from the pockets of students around the room. But he could see that he was three clunks away from getting out of there. Ty was saying something to him, but he had stopped listening. Two clunks. "Sure," he replied. "Whatever." One clunk.

"All right, clath," Mrs. Weaver broke in. The bell rang and the noise level rose instantly. "Thee you next week." The teacher unrolled a huge wad of tissue, smashed it into her face, and trumpeted a deafening sneeze into it.

"Good grief," Presley groaned. "If we have to face germ warfare then I'm wearing a hazmat suit next week." She gathered up her books. "Thanks for looking all that stuff up and taking all those notes," she said sweetly, flashing a shy smile at Tiberius. "See you guys tomorrow." And Presley darted off.

Tomorrow? Trace had missed something.

"And be on time, please." Kali sighed. She did not look at Trace or Ty but slung her book bag over her shoulder, lifting her braids from under its strap before sailing off to join friends who waited for her by the door.

"Tomorrow, what?" Trace asked.

"The library?" Tiberius raised his eyebrows. "We're meeting at one p.m., right?" He paused. "You said it was cool, dude." Tiberius looked a little annoyed.

"Yeah, sure," Trace bluffed, "one o'clock sharp. Over on Clinton Street, right?"

"No, man. NYPL main," Tiberius said. "The one with the lions? The big building on Forty-Second and Fifth?" He packed up his book bag, carefully sliding his pad in between his heavily illustrated notebooks. "You okay, Trace?" he asked.

"Duh-UH," Trace said. "Just messing with you, man." He poked Ty in the ribs and they headed for the door. One o'clock would be tricky. Even if the subway ran on time, it ran slowly on weekends. Maybe if he had a legitimate reason, and research for a school assignment was seriously legit, maybe the doctor could finish shrinking his head a little early tomorrow.

# 4

It had been a rough night. There was the dream, of course. There was always the dream. But the strong dark hands that were yanking him from the car had been so insistent this time that Trace awoke rubbing his forearms and, still sleepy, had even checked them for bruises. He was burning up.

It was five a.m. Too early to get up, but if he went back to sleep he risked going back to the river. Asleep, the waters might overtake him again, choking off his air. Awake, thoughts of *why* and *I shoulda* and *if only* would stoke the hot ache in his chest until *that* suffocated him.

Trace kicked off the covers. Stretching his legs to

the ceiling, he let it cool the soles of his feet. And he thought about smiles. What was that smile that Presley had given Tiberius? Had that meant something? Girls smiled for too many reasons. Trace followed the thought, putting some distance between his mind and the river. His legs felt cooler now. Maybe she had a crush on Ty?

Presley Jackson had skipped a grade, which meant she must be smart, but the whole class treated her like a ditzy kid sister. No one teased her or gave her any attitude, they just didn't take her seriously. She was cute. But cute like lion-cub cute or koala-bear cute. He couldn't guess what her parents must be: she was caramel colored, green-eyed, and kinda Asian looking . . . but not. Trace laughed softly in the darkness. The girl had *no* figure yet. What was she? Like twelve? Probably too much woman for Ty. He laughed again.

He was actually feeling cold now. Dropping back under the covers, he gave himself a few minutes to enjoy the warmth; then, unwilling to risk falling asleep again, he climbed down from the bed to get ready. *Carpe the diem*, Auntie Lea liked to say. Seize the day.

❋❋❋

Dr. Proctor's office was on the first floor of a tidy brownstone on a leafy street in the Clinton Hill section of Brooklyn. It was only blocks from his aunt's apartment, but a world apart all the same. Here, gracious town houses were not necessarily broken up into tiny apartments. Most had only one doorbell and shaded driveways and nannies to help the toddlers who lived in them navigate around the stone planters decorating their front steps.

After his parents' funeral, when Trace had come to live with her, Auntie Lea had first suggested, then insisted, that he talk to a therapist. Trace had not wanted to talk to anybody. But seeing a stranger once a week had seemed a lot easier than explaining to his aunt why he did not want to talk to her about his "feelings." So Auntie Lea paid for one hour of Dr. Proctor's time every Saturday.

It was on his third visit that he had run into Yolanda Stringer in the narrow hallway of the building. She was slouching down the stairs, rolling her eyes as her mother, standing on the landing above, called out a list of groceries for her to remember. Yolanda had looked over his head at the sign on the doctor's door, then leveled her gaze on him almost triumphantly and snorted. She had something on him. And Trace never had to wonder how it was that everyone at school seemed to know his business.

"Come on in, Theo," Dr. Dorothea Proctor said now, stepping into her small waiting room just as he arrived. On his first visit, the doctor's name had seemed ridiculous. He had spent the whole hour pretending to think about her questions, but really, he had been cataloging words besides *doctor* that rhymed with Proctor: Rock more. Lock door.

And although the tall, round-faced doctor looked and sounded Jamaican and had curiously muscular arms like a weight lifter and was wearing an engagement ring at their first meeting but not now, Trace knew he was not there to ask *her* any questions.

"How was your week, Theo?" Dr. Proctor began.

"Fine," he said. "Just fine." They did this every Saturday. He said "fine, just fine" to almost every question while she made notes or tapped a pen on her knee for an hour.

"Okay, then I guess I'll see you next week," the doctor said.

Trace had been slumped on a small leather couch next to the armchair where the doctor sat. Now he sat up straight. "I can go?"

Dr. Proctor just smiled at him.

"I don't get it," he said. Trace thought about Ty and the girls he had to meet at the library. He would be early. And here he had been worried about having to listen to Kali say something nasty if he showed up a minute late.

"Seriously?" he asked.

Dr. Proctor just nodded.

Trace was up in a flash and at the door. He had his hand on the doorknob. "This is a trick, right?" he asked, looking over his shoulder. "To get me to talk about it, huh?"

Dr. Proctor said nothing. Her face was a blank.

Would she tell Auntie Lea he had ducked out after five minutes? Would *he* tell? Trace held the doorknob. That wave began rolling over him again, but gently. What was the big deal about talking? Why would Auntie Lea pay real money she needed for other stuff so that he could sit here and play this game of tag every week? And now Dr. Proctor was trying to change the rules. The wave subsided but the smell of the river was there, making him feel a little light-headed.

"Okay. Look," Trace said quietly. He walked back to the couch and sank weakly into its soft leather cushions. "We can talk a little, okay?" He looked up at the doctor, but her expression did not change. "A little. 'Cause I really do need to leave early today." Trace waited, but she said nothing.

With some effort, he continued. "You keep asking how I *feel* every week." The doctor nodded.

"But I don't." Trace took in a slow breath and let it out. "I don't feel."

"Everyone *feels*, Theo," the doctor said. "Even if that feeling is emptiness or . . ." The doctor seemed to be looking for a word, but her pause went on forever.

"Or . . . guilt?" Theo asked in a near whisper.

"Do you feel *guilty*, Theo?" The doctor frowned slightly. "Accidents happen. You had no control over what happened, you know that, don't you?" She leaned forward in her chair, her moonlike face clouded over now. Trace studied her eyes.

At their very first meeting she had promised that whatever he told her would be private, just between them. So maybe he could tell her about being in the car, about his dad swerving to miss a deer on the road that evening. He might even tell her about his mom screaming. His mom. Screaming. She had been terrified but still trying to reassure him. Or he could tell her about his dad's kicking. But all that kicking did not crack one car window or make one door budge as the car was sinking, so what was the point of talking about it? They were gone.

"Theo?" Dr. Proctor said gently. "You do know that nothing that happened that night was your fault?"

Trace looked up at her. Doctors didn't know everything. In fact, they didn't know much at all. Because they shouldn't have been on that road at that time in the evening when that stupid deer ran out of the stupid trees. No wonder people shot them. If somebody had shot that deer, it wouldn't have been there and his dad would have just kept driving. Trace felt something thick and wet and too large stuck in his throat. The lump wouldn't go down but he tried several times to swallow. "We'll be home before dark, kiddo." That was the last thing his dad had said before the deer. "Home before dark."

"Theodore?" the doctor asked once more. Now she looked worried. "Is everything okay?"

Trace was back on that road. Back in the car. It was all his fault that they were there at that exact time, and he would always know that. For as long as he lived. That lump of river would be there forever too, even if he somehow forgot about it for a minute, it would still be there, waiting. He looked into Dr. Proctor's eyes.

"Fine," he said. "Just fine."

5

Trace had polished off two cartons of orange juice on the train ride into Manhattan. They had successfully washed away the taste of the river, but now he needed to find a bathroom. He was not sure where to find the Rose Main Reading Room or the men's room once he reached the library, so he was glad that he had arrived early.

The wide stone steps in front of the New York Public Library were dotted with all types of people reading and chatting or maybe just waiting for something. After the morning's chill, it had turned out to be a sunny October day, perfect for lingering on the steps. But Trace had only enough time to find the john before finding the Reading Room where he was to meet Ty and the girls.

He nodded at Patience and Fortitude, the massive marble lions on either side of the steps. When he had told Auntie Lea that he planned to meet his study group at the library after seeing Dr. Proctor, she had told him the lions' names and asked that he give them her regards. Trace wondered why people said that. What were regards? For that matter, why were twin lions outside of a library? To guard it? Who were they protecting it from . . . crazed readers? The way they stared down their noses at the crowd jostling along Fifth Avenue, Trace thought they might be better named Bored and Snooty.

He took the steps two at a time, happy to think about anything but the doctor's questions. The subway ride had been nice and noisy: a flute player walking through cars with a paper cup full of money tied to his waist, a tattooed couple arguing loudly about which stop was closest to their friend's place, a fat little kid banging into passengers and refusing to sit no matter what his mother said. Any distraction was good.

At the entrance to the library, a couple of tourists were quizzing the guard for directions, so Trace

42

waited. He *really* had to go. By the time the *brain-dead* couple *finally* grasped that street numbers got higher going uptown—*duh*—and lower—*ya think*?—if they went downtown, Trace was afraid he would pop. At last, it was his turn and the guard pointed him toward a staircase that led down to the toilets. Trace ran for it.

Ten minutes later, he was ready. He was on time, early even, and nothing Kali could say would rattle him. They had picked which events they each would cover, so today was just about research and getting an outline together. Besides, he was pretty sure everyone had to be absolutely quiet in this library. If Kali did start anything, a guard would probably toss her butt out. Trace smiled at the thought and checked himself in the bathroom mirror. His mom always said he looked very handsome in this buttery-yellow shirt. She said it made his skin look like "polished mahogany." Or sometimes she'd say, "like sweet warm cocoa, Teddy."

Mom. When had he made her stop calling him Teddy Bear? When had it changed to Teddy? *My Teddy Bear.* Mom's hands tucking the covers under his chin, her soft kiss on his cheek. Trace closed his eyes and tried to swallow. The lump in his throat had returned.

No. He was not going down that road. He turned the water on full blast in the sink, let it run over his hands for a minute, then splashed his face once, twice. He would *not* think about it. Not now. He dried his hands and face quickly and hurried out of the men's room.

Hiking his book bag over his shoulder, Trace fumbled through his jacket pockets for his phone as he barreled along the hallway. He had three minutes to find the Reading Room. He saw a text message from Ty that must have just come in: *dude theyre here. where r u?* Trace grinned. Tiberius was surrounded and panicking. It was time to go play cavalry.

He passed more doors on his way out than he had on his way in, but Trace wouldn't realize that until later. Hurrying along an empty corridor, he looked up from his phone and saw a stairwell he hadn't noticed before. But it led down. So he retraced his steps.

"I only came down one level," he whispered to himself. Trace stopped and tried to get his bearings. To his right and left, the hall was empty and as silent as a tomb. The few doors he saw were closed. The emptiness spooked him, but just for a minute. "Duh, it's *Saturday*," he said aloud, surprised as the sound of his voice was magnified by the marble floors and walls. "And *why* am I whispering?"

Where was the up staircase? Trace suddenly felt annoyed. He was going to be late. And if Kali said one negative word or rolled her eyes or started any trouble at all, he was not going to take it. The hall he was in led to another corridor that looked exactly the same, so, doubling back to the stairs he had seen, he took them down, hoping to find an elevator.

When he reached the bottom of the stairs, Trace found he was in a vast, open, and dimly lit room filled with so many rows of bookshelves that he could not see where they ended. The walls down here were patchworks of old brick, dusty in places with plaster and scratches. It was too shadowy and cold, and Trace knew with a sudden certainty that he was not meant to see the books that filled the shelves before him. It was like peeking behind the curtain in Oz. Even in the little light available, the spines of the books on every shelf looked old and fragile. Trace felt like an intruder. As he turned to go back up the stairs he saw an exit sign just to his left. Excellent.

The shadows darkened and the floor sloped as he headed toward it, but he saw that there was an opening ahead. Suddenly, he felt weirdly electrified. Even through the thickness of his jacket and shirt he could feel the hairs on his arms standing on end. *It must be the chill down here*, he thought. If this floor were unused on weekends, of course they would not heat it. Or maybe the weirdness came from the dead silence? Trace realized that he had been tiptoeing toward the opening, and, trying to shake off what he was feeling, he picked up speed. To his relief, there was an elevator door just beyond the exit sign, and, more importantly, there was an Up button next to it. Trace exhaled, only then aware that he had been holding his breath.

His finger was inches from the button when he heard it: crying. He froze. If it was possible for silence to grow deeper, it did. Every nerve in Trace's body was awake and waiting. He heard it again. A whimper. Someone was down there with him. Trace pushed the elevator button, trying to stay calm. The button lit up. He held his breath.

There it was again. This time, he recognized that it was a child crying. A little kid was down there, lost just like he was. A long run of sobs followed, louder now and punctuated by choppy intakes of air. Oh, man. There was no time for this. Above the elevator, the letter *G* lit up. It was on the ground floor. The elevator was coming.

On an impulse, Trace took a quick look around the corner. The rows of shelves disappeared into darkness. If the place gave *him* the creeps, he could not imagine that a child would willingly hide down here in the darkness. But all the same, there it was again: a pitiful little sob. Trace could almost see the runny nose that would come with it.

"Hey," he called out softly. "What's the matter?" The crying stopped. Trace took a step toward the shelves. From behind a stack that was only feet away, he heard a trembling whimper. His own heart was beating so loudly that he almost missed it.

"C'mon, kid," he said gently. "Come on out, I'll help you find your mom." The elevator dinged loudly and Trace jumped. As the doors opened, Trace ran and put his book bag on the floor to keep them from closing. He was officially late now. Ty was probably pissed.

Trace turned around. Standing just beyond the opening in front of the nearest bookcase was a little boy. The red light from the exit sign mixed with the darkness, turning his skin the color of raisins, but his face was in shadow. As small as he was, he could not have been more than four years old. Trace felt a flush of anger. People should keep an eye on their kids. This was ridiculous. "Come on, kid," he said, trying not to sound impatient. "The guard upstairs will find your mommy."

The child stayed in the shadows. Trace frowned. The kid was a mess. Even in such dim light, it was clear that his clothes were tattered, his hair was a wild rat's nest of tangles, and the ragged shoes he wore barely covered his feet. And, sure enough, the kid's nose was running like a faucet.

"*C'mon*, kid," Trace said again. This was nuts. He was not going to chase the boy. If he would not come, he would just tell one of the guards where to find the kid. Stepping into the elevator, Trace slung his backpack over his shoulder again and held the door open with one hand. "Last chance," he said. "I'll go tell your mom and she'll come get you, okay?"

Kids heard the slogan "Stranger Danger" all the time, so he could not blame the little guy for not coming to him. If he tried to grab him, the kid might freak out. Crying was one thing. But dragging along somebody's kid who was screaming bloody murder would be more drama than he had time for.

"*Okaaaay* . . . ," he said, drawing it out to give the boy another minute. He heard a soft shushing, the sound of little feet moving over concrete. The boy inched forward out of the shadow.

Trace jerked backward, his hand flying off the elevator door. It was that boy he had seen outside the deli. The doors began to close. How was that even possible?

He stabbed at the elevator button and the steel doors obeyed, shuddering open again. The boy's large, dark eyes were trained on his. At least, it *looked* like the same boy.

Suddenly Trace felt a deep sadness wash over him, like his whole body was crying. He knew he should be freaking out, but all he felt was . . . sorry. Even if this was the same kid . . . and no way *could* it be . . . how could anyone be so careless with such a little guy or bring him to the library looking so shabby?

"Stay right here, little man," Trace said softly, trying to sound reassuring. "Your mom will come for you, okay?" He punched the G button and the doors began to close. The little boy began backing away toward the shelves. His eyes were huge and they never left Trace's. The crack of space between the doors was shrinking.

In the glow of the red light, Trace saw that the boy's dark eyes were shiny with tears. But, as the doors closed, what he also saw . . . what he could *not* have really seen . . . were the books on the shelf behind the boy. The little boy was looking right at him. And Trace could see right through him.

# 6

"Okay, tell me one more time, Mr. Goody-Good Samaritan. Yer aunt's on her way but we got plenny a time."

The badge stuck to the guard's chest read *Lemuel T. Spitz*. That name was bad enough. But from where Trace sat, looking up over the ridge of Lemuel's mountainous gut, that didn't seem to be the worst of it. The man's face looked like cold pizza after it had been picked clean of pepperoni: *very* waxy, *very* cratered, and punctuated with unhealthy-looking patches of pink. Unfortunately, Trace also had an excellent view up into Lemuel's cavernous nostrils, a sight he would not easily forget.

There seemed to be no point in going over it again.

Trace had grabbed the first guard he saw, told him about the kid, and now here he sat, forty-five minutes and three guards later, in the security office. The guard had accompanied him back downstairs, but the elevator door had only opened once the guard inserted his key into a panel of buttons. Problem number one: the guard did not believe Trace had merely walked downstairs into the area.

Problem two: when Trace showed the guard where he had last seen the boy, the kid was nowhere to be found. Trace called out, the guard called out. And then the guard unclipped a little two-way radio from his belt and barked a code into it. Two more guards appeared and lights were switched on, the rows of shelves bathing the whole floor in even deeper shadows. They had marched Trace around a city block's worth of dusty shelves and dark corridors, but there was no child to be found.

"Maybe the kid took the same stairs I did and has already found his mom," Trace had offered.

"The public's not allowed down here," one guard said firmly, scowling at Trace in the harsh overhead light. "You did *not* just walk down the stairs to this floor." But he had. Hadn't he?

"Well . . . maybe his mom came and . . . and she found him," Trace added weakly. He did not believe it himself. He was not at all sure now how he had found his way down there if it was a locked area. The air was musty and cold still, but different now. The electricity he had felt before was missing. The boy was gone.

But that didn't matter because the guards were not listening to him anyway. They seemed to have reached some agreement, or maybe they had a rule for what to do when someone reports a missing kid who *then* goes missing. *Fine*, Trace thought. *Don't believe me.* Suddenly, he remembered his dad saying, "No good deed goes unpunished." That had never made sense to him before, but now Trace got it. Forget he had said anything. He just wanted to go find his friends, if they were even still there.

But the guards had encircled him on the elevator ride back upstairs, then walked him like a prisoner through the lobby and across to the security office without another word. It was a small, ugly office too, considering all the carved marble and polished brass that lay beyond its door in the library. The few chairs and desks it held looked battered and grimy. Gray metal file cabinets stood on either side of the door, their sagging drawers sporting plastic-covered labels too cloudy to read. Lemuel T. Spitz had been waiting for him.

"I didn't do anything," Trace protested. "I have to go meet my friends." He glared at the three guards, but they were already halfway out the door, leaving Trace to tell his story to Spitz . . . repeatedly. It was ridiculous.

Lemuel T. Spitz had taken Trace's name and address, and then his cell phone . . . like he was under arrest or might call for a getaway car. Then the man had called Auntie Lea and asked her to come in because they were holding him for "questioning." Trace couldn't imagine what she must be thinking. He knew she had a photo shoot today for a music magazine and he was pretty sure that dropping everything to come retrieve him would be a huge pain. The way Spitz had snarled on the phone, she probably thought he had been caught stealing something.

Trace was no angel. He knew that. But he always *tried* to do the right thing. And he had tried especially hard not to cause problems for his aunt. Had he taken

one shot at any of the guys at school who "accidentally" rammed his shoulder or drove an elbow into his
ribs as they passed in the halls? No. Did he bust the
girl in algebra who kept leaning across the aisle to
copy his papers? No. He had held his tongue. Held his
fists. He had allowed more than a few taunts to slam
into the mask he wore and never said one word. Nasty
comments had sizzled on the surface or even dug clean
through that mask, but he had been cool. Auntie Lea
probably felt she was already carrying extra weight
with him around. And now this.

"Can I have my phone back?" Trace asked, as evenly
and politely as he could. "Please," he added.

Spitz snorted. But before he could answer, a tall
black man in a denim shirt poked his head in the door.
Glancing around, he came in, picked up the worst-
looking chair in the room, and then set it outside the
door. "Where's that table with the cracked leg?" he
asked Spitz. The guard pointed to a small table piled
high with folders, coffee cups, bulging key rings, man-
uals, and one gray potted cactus. The man raised an
eyebrow and looked at Spitz expectantly.

"C'mon. You see I'm doin' an *investigation* here,

Dallas," Spitz drawled. "Can'tcha just pile that stuff on a shelf for me, for Chrissake?"

The man rolled his eyes slightly and Trace thought he saw the man give him the slightest wink. Shaking his head, the man began moving things off the table and wedging them into any space he could find on desktops or shelves. Spitz went into overdrive now that he had an audience.

"Now, *allegedly*, Mr. Theodore Carter, you claim you came upon an underage minor who you ascertained to be lost in the stacks." Spitz leaned over him menacingly as he spoke.

"The stacks?" Trace asked.

"The stacks, downstairs where you were—the stacks," Spitz said impatiently. "Thass what they're called down there. All them stacks of old books. And *you*, mister"—Spitz pointed a meaty finger in his face—"you had no business down there at all." With that, Spitz leaned back and stuck his thumbs up under his belly to hook them, with some effort, onto his belt. Maybe it was his too-tight uniform or the steam hissing from the vent by the desk, or possibly it was because his audience was ignoring his performance, but Lemuel T. Spitz's face was growing pinker and moister by the second.

Trace didn't have time for this. By now, Tiberius would be ready to boil him in oil. In as polite a tone as he could manage, he told Spitz his story one more time: He had taken a wrong turn and was trying to get back to the lobby when he heard crying. He saw a little black boy, maybe three or four years old tops, wearing raggedy clothes, his hair uncombed, busted-up shoes, big eyes. He told Spitz everything. Well, not *everything*.

"Hold it, will you?" asked the tall man. He was carrying the table with both hands and stood waiting by the door. It took both Trace and the guard a few beats to realize the man was talking about the door and not about the TV-cop-style questioning Spitz was conducting.

Lemuel T. Spitz yanked his thumbs free and, scowling as though he had been interrupted just on the brink of getting a confession, he opened the door. As the man maneuvered the table through the door, Trace could see his aunt in the vast hall beyond it, being pointed toward the security office. This was really bad.

Auntie Lea was getting dropped in the deep end of parenting and Trace knew that, at best, she must be struggling just to tread water. She had never been a parent. She hadn't read the Mom Playbook or anything close to it. So bedtime had been *mentioned* when he first arrived, but she never noticed when or even if he had actually turned in. The first three days he had been in Brooklyn she had actually fixed him breakfast. But he saw that getting up before noon was torture for her, and neither one of them wanted to keep up the performance. He offered to just find something in the fridge. She offered ten bucks every morning so he could grab breakfast on his way to school. They managed. Trace found he was on his own with laundry, showers, homework, haircuts—all the stuff that had to be at critical mass before he would have gotten around to it *before*. Before. Auntie Lea just wasn't wired to play mom. With no prep time at all, she was suddenly IT. Maybe this would be more than she could handle. Maybe this was too much? Definitely, Trace decided. Way too much.

He could barely look up as Auntie Lea knocked, then opened the door wide. Her eyes were dark under a knit cap pulled low on her forehead and Trace could almost see heat waves trembling the air around her. She stood stock-still in the doorway, one hand clenched on the doorknob. Auntie Lea took in the dingy little office, then turned to study the sweating, bubblegum-pink-faced guard in the too-tight uniform hunched over Trace. Lemuel T. Spitz never knew what hit him.

## 7

Somewhere, sometime, Trace had heard that the scent of vanilla had a calming effect on the nervous system. Steam was rising from the pot of hot chocolate that Auntie Lea was stirring on the stove. She had laced it with cinnamon, nutmeg, and, yes, vanilla. But the whole calming thing was not working.

Trace chewed on the inside of his lip. Auntie Lea had blown into the kitchen, whipped off her jacket, scrubbed her hands furiously at the kitchen sink, and slammed a pot onto the stove. She had been muttering all the time, shaking her head, in conversation with *someone*. Trace had never seen her like this. So he was trying to be there, ready for what was coming, and, at the same time, *not* be there.

Auntie Lea had barely spoken since they left the library, although she had had quite a bit to say to Lemuel T. Spitz. It seemed that criminology was one of her lesser-known -ologies, because the string of legalese that she had unleashed almost made Trace feel sorry for the guard. She had gone total *CSI* on Spitz: words like *unlawful detention* and *underage minor* and *coercion* had bounced off the walls of the dreary little office. A spoon banged loudly against the stovetop as Auntie Lea stepped up her stirring . . . and muttering. His turn was coming.

Trace studied the single gray, stick-thin tree in the backyard outside the tall kitchen window. A squirrel spiraled his way down the trunk, looked around nervously, and darted off into the bushes. *Good move*, Trace thought. *You don't want to stick around for this*. But he hadn't *done* anything. Auntie Lea had not even asked him his version of what had happened. She had let Spitz sputter on and on about *trespassing* and *suspicious behavior* and all the *man-hours* lost looking into a *false report*. Steam coated the kitchen window and everything beyond it looked hazy now. Where would he go if Auntie Lea had had it with him? Trace scratched a fingernail along a seam in the wooden tabletop, trying to pry up a splinter.

His mom had said once, no, had said *many* times that he needed to try extra hard to see things from other people's points of view. Being an only child could make you selfish. It could make you think that you were the center of the universe. It could make you inconsiderate of what other people needed, she said. He didn't feel inconsiderate. He had tried to stay out of Auntie Lea's way. Tried to keep his bed neat, if not completely made up. His desk wasn't that messy and he usually washed any dishes he used. He had thought about Auntie Lea a lot. A *lot*. He never asked for money, or for new clothes, or to go to the movies. He didn't talk her head off or complain about things at school. He never brought any friends, well, Tiberius, home with him. Nothing. He just should have found Tiberius and the girls and never said a word to that guard.

The yard looked even colder now that Trace was thinking he might be leaving. Auntie Lea grew quiet as she began pouring cocoa into two huge, mismatched mugs she had made in a pottery class, then dusted a bit more cinnamon over each. Everything about the kitchen suddenly seemed warm: the amber light that fell across the table, the oleander tree in the corner, hung with pink blossoms that seemed to ignore the calendar, the chocolate-vanilla air that should have been soothing . . . but wasn't.

"Okay," Auntie Lea said slowly. She set a steaming mug in front of Trace and sat down opposite him, resting her elbows on the table and leaning forward to slowly inhale the aroma rising from her own cup. Trace bit hard on the inside of his lip. Could he guarantee her that this would never happen again? That she would not have to leave a job to come bail him out or clean up some stupid mess that he never saw coming? Looking at things from her side, playing mom was too much work.

"What exactly happened?" she asked.

Trace studied his hands. They looked detached and clumsy, wrapped around the mug. The cup was too hot, but he left his hands there and focused on the burn. Appreciated it, even. Because if he looked into Auntie Lea's eyes, those eyes that were his mother's eyes, it would hurt more. Where exactly was left to go? Trace saw it now: this whole time had been a test, a trial period, and he should have done better. He was extra food and piles of paperwork. He was school meetings and doctor visits. Auntie Lea had no privacy. Could she go out of town? Or hang out with friends? Not with a kid around. Trace looked up at his aunt. He hadn't done anything wrong. But he should have tried harder to do something right.

"I was supposed to meet Ty and the girls in my study group," he began. "But I went downstairs to the washroom first." Trace blew on his cocoa. He wanted to be honest. So he told her about arriving early at the library, taking a wrong turn, seeing the boy. But some things he left out, like cutting out on therapy, being in an off-limits area, seeing a boy down there that he could swear he had seen the day before. Trace took a deep breath. And seeing right *through* him. Even he didn't believe that part. An invisible kid. How many more therapists would it take to explain that one?

"I thought I should tell the guards, but the kid must've left," he finished. Trace felt drained. His aunt was angry, Ty was probably angry, and Kali now had proof that he was a screw-up. He blew across his cocoa again then sipped it, feeling warm and calmer somehow as he drank. Auntie Lea was watching him.

"I was furious," she said quietly. "I know I lost my temper with that man, and I'm sorry you had to see that. But I am sick of the way some of these overbearing, insecure, hide-behind-a-uniform, wannabe petty tyrants try to intimidate young black males at every opportunity." Auntie Lea's eyebrows knit together as she slowly stirred what was left of her cocoa. "He had no right to detain you. No right to take your cell phone." She looked out of the kitchen window and began stirring more vigorously.

"I should call a lawyer is what I should do," she said, almost to herself. "The nerve of that guy! Here you are trying to help *them* out. Shoot! They leave doors unlocked so kids can wander off and get lost. And they never even found the child, did they? What is wrong with those people? Security, my butt!" Auntie Lea was shaking her head now, not really talking to him anymore. She banged her spoon around inside her mug. "Suspicious? They called *you* suspicious? I got your suspicious! I oughta—"

"Auntie Lea," Trace interrupted. "I . . . I'm really sorry you had to come to the library like that. I know you were on that job today. . . ." To his surprise, his aunt's mood shifted immediately. Putting her spoon down, she turned and smiled at him as though he had just arrived.

"Nothing," she said, leaning toward him, "and I mean *nothing*, is more important to me than you, Theo." She studied his face thoughtfully. "You and I are family, okay? Family looks out for family." She reached out and held her hand gently against his face.

"I thought . . . ," Trace said. But what he had been thinking he did not want to hear himself say out loud.

"Finish your cocoa, mister," Auntie Lea said brightly, pushing away from the table. "I'll be right back." With that, his aunt hurried out of the kitchen, stirring up the scent of cinnamon in the air as she left.

Trace looked again at the yard. The squirrel was back, perched on a branch of the thin gray tree and looking right at him. *It's his tree*, Trace thought, shaking his head. Even squirrels live *somewhere*. Dipping his spoon into the cocoa, he scooped up the warm chocolate that had settled at the bottom and licked it clean. It was funny, but he could still feel the warmth of his aunt's hand on his face. Something like the wave had come with her touch. But this one was a gentle wave, Trace thought, and not bad at all.

✳✳✳

"Look at all this stuff," Auntie Lea said. She was out of breath and threads of cobwebs clung to her hair. She held an overstuffed straw basket in her arms that looked like it was ready to fall apart. With a huff, she landed it on the table in front of him. "Ready?" she asked.

Trace had no idea what to say, so he just nodded.

"Okay, it's time. I haven't been through all this stuff, but we should do it together," Auntie Lea said. "Need more cocoa?" She looked at him expectantly.

"I'm good," Trace said. "What is all this?"

"I had this stuff in the basement. I brought it all back from Aunt Frenchy's funeral." Auntie Lea began pulling out photo albums, small cloth bags, handfuls of jewelry, several framed pictures, chipped, rusty, and dusty things he could not identify, and arranged everything neatly on the kitchen table. His aunt was watching him as though she suspected he might detonate at any moment. They had not talked about his great-aunt's funeral. They had not talked about anything that might even remind him of that time. And now Auntie Lea was talking way too cheerily and way too fast.

"Look at all this stuff," Auntie Lea said. "Aunt

Frenchy was too much! You know her real name was Françoise, right? I think she could count to ten in French and maybe ask where a bathroom was, but that was it. What a character. My aunt, your *great-*aunt Françoise. I don't think anyone ever called her anything but Frenchy, though." Auntie Lea laughed just a little and coughed. "Good grief, this stuff is dusty! We should clean it all up though, you know? No telling what's in here, but Mom wanted me and Savannah to have this." She looked up at Trace.

Savannah. So there it was. Trace had not heard his mother's name spoken since his parents' funeral. They were going back *there*. They were going to have to talk about it. It took Trace only seconds to understand that this was what the trouble at the library was going to cost him. Auntie Lea wanted in, she wanted in. She was no longer just a caretaker. He would no longer be just a guest in need of a place to stay. *Family looks out for family*. Auntie Lea wanted to be close. Close like he had been with his mom and dad. He might want that too. But there was really no way to tell her everything.

Trace could smell the mustiness rising from the basket and its contents, which spread across the table. The photo albums had water stains and frayed edges and corners of yellowed papers crumbling between faded black pages. No telling what was in the cloth bags. But a rust-colored dust had settled on the table around everything. That mustiness began filling the room. He recognized the sickly sweet, foul green scent of the river bottom. And under it was the faint milky aroma of chocolate that lingered . . . was it coming from his mug? Was it coating his lips? It made his head swim.

"Theo?" his aunt said gently. "You okay?"

The doorbell buzzed loudly and Trace jumped. "I-I'll get it," he stammered, escaping to the front door before his aunt could say a word. A worn lace curtain covered the small window in the front door and through it he could see the back of a girl's head. She looked too small to be a Jehovah's Witness. Girl Scout cookies? The wrong doorbell? Trace swung the door open and a rush of cool air hit him, clearing his head as the girl turned around.

"Presley?" Trace blinked. How did she even know where he lived? Swinging a backpack off her shoulders, the girl cheerfully pushed past him into the hallway.

"Ty *totally* fulminated," she said. "You got snacks?"

8

Lured by the fragrance of chocolate, Presley had made her way to the kitchen before Trace could say another word. *Fulminated* was rattling around in his brain as he watched the girl make herself at home at the table.

"I'm Presley Jackson," she was explaining to Auntie Lea. "Trace picked me to be in his study posse at school." Not entirely accurate, and very oddly put, Trace thought, but his aunt looked so delighted—and so distracted from the piles on the table—that he did not correct her.

"I'm Leatrice Cumberbatch, Theo's . . . um . . . Trace's aunt. Could I interest you in some hot chocolate?" Auntie Lea asked, giving Trace a wink as though she approved of this pipsqueak who must be his secret crush.

"I was interested in chocolate before I was born," Presley chirped. Auntie Lea shot a questioning glance at Trace, but he could only shrug.

"So what do you mean, 'fulminated,' Presley? What's up with Ty?"

"He's exacerbated, chafed, totally incensed—you know, he fulminated," she answered. "I mean he was really, really steamed when you didn't show up and I said, 'Hey, give the guy a break, things happen,' but Ty was all, like, 'I can't believe he blew off this meeting,' and I said, 'Well, just text him and see what's going on,' and he said, 'I did,' all hostile, so I said, 'Fine!' and he said 'Fine!' and I figured I'd email you and tell you what we did." Presley took a breath. "But then when I asked for your address . . . as in, *duh*, email address . . . he told me where you actually *lived* lived, and I live, like, two blocks over, unreal, right? And Ty was all *churlish* about even talking to me since I was on your side and he acted like he was doing me a big favor, so thank you very much, I don't *think* so, Mr. Bellicose." Presley rolled her eyes dramatically.

"Okay," said Trace slowly. There were sides to take

now? He had planned to call Ty when he got home. He felt sure it would be easy to straighten out what had happened, but Presley showing up like this was entirely too weird.

Auntie Lea handed Presley a mug of hot chocolate and became absorbed in reading the metal buttons that were studding her backpack. *Go Green or Go Home*, *I ♥ Tattoos*, *Peace, Love & Pastries*, they shouted. Some had images of insects and rap stars and heavily frosted cupcakes. Just the usual mix, Trace thought. The kid was nuts.

"So what did I miss?" he asked her, bracing for another oddly phrased flood of words. It took a while, and an additional mug of hot chocolate with a side of ginger cookies, for Presley to download the Post-it's worth of information about what the group had accomplished. They had each noted resources for their topics that were better found in the library than online and they had agreed to meet after school on Tuesday to map out their presentation. Trace stole a look at the clock on the stove. It was nearly five p.m. Surely Presley needed to head home before it got dark.

"Thank you for the delicious snacks, Ms. Cumberbatch, but I have to go," she said suddenly, giving Trace a small frown, almost as if she had read his mind.

"Take some cookies with you if you like," Auntie Lea offered.

Presley brightened. She folded three cookies into a napkin and opened her backpack to fit them in. A book slid out. *Word Power Made Easy*. So that was it. It had to be tough to be younger than everyone else in class. But Trace would not be the one to tell her that all her big words just sounded loony, laughable, and ludicrous. He caught himself smiling.

"What *is* all this old stuff anyway?" Presley asked, slipping her backpack on. She leaned over the table, seeming to have just noticed the piles in front of her. Picking up a strand of glass beads, she held them up to the light. "Cool," she breathed.

"We were just going through some things that my aunt Frenchy left me when you arrived," Auntie Lea explained. Presley nodded.

She opened a photo album and some of the black paper crumbled on her fingers. "Oh, wow! Sorry, Ms. Cumberbatch, I really—" she said.

"Don't worry about it, dear." Auntie Lea smiled. "It's all pretty old and falling apart. We're just sorting through it."

Trace watched Presley. She seemed genuinely interested. It would be nice to be able to look at these family relics like a stranger might. Not to feel there were land mines in the pile. Her fingers were running over brooches and bracelets, a crinkled fan, a carved ivory box.

"Yeowwwch!" Presley gasped. She had picked up a metal object that was shaped like a little mallet. But she dropped it instantly and it landed with a clattering rattle on the table.

"Are you okay?" Auntie Lea asked, hurrying around the table to take Presley's hand. "What happened? Did you get a splinter?"

Presley looked at her fingers, then at Auntie Lea, then at Trace. "It burned," she said quietly. She looked confused, but there was something more, Trace thought.

"What do you mean, 'burned'?" he asked. "Is that another one of your synonyms for something?" He did not like what he saw in her eyes. She looked almost afraid.

Presley shook her head. "I . . . I've got to go," she said, ignoring his comment about her choice of words. "Sorry. It was nice meeting you, Ms. Cumberbatch." She turned and headed toward the door. Trace could only shrug when Auntie Lea made a questioning face at him. She had picked up the little metal object and was turning it over in her hands, inspecting it for any sharp ragged edges or protruding sliver of metal.

Trace caught up to Presley at the front door.

"Thanks for coming by, Presley," he said. "Really." She looked up at him nervously. "Do you want some lotion or something for your fingers, maybe?" he asked.

"No, thanks," she said. "Bye." And then she was off, down the front stairs and hurrying away from the building as though he was radioactive.

"Weird," Trace said. He studied the sky. The air was crisp and carried the faint smell of wood burning in a fireplace. A police siren screamed in the distance. He would never, ever in a trillion years understand girls. They had on and off switches that flipped easily, and it was never clear what did it. He shivered in the chill wind as he watched Presley round the corner onto Myrtle Avenue. Closing the door, Trace headed back to the kitchen, ready to face Aunt Frenchy's souvenirs. But Auntie Lea was putting the last of the pile back into the basket.

"We'll go through this old stuff later," she said. "I'm starving. Gotta get some dinner going."

The little metal object was still on the table.

"What is that thing?" he asked.

"Looks like an old toy," Auntie Lea answered. She picked it up and turned it around and around in her hands. "Some kind of whistle, maybe. But a rattle too, see?" She gave it a shake and the sound of dry seeds loose in a tin can prickled his ears. The sound made him uneasy.

"Hey, don't you have homework to do?" Auntie Lea asked. "Get busy and I'll call you when dinner's ready, okay?" She dropped the rattle into the basket with the rest of the stuff.

"I'm feeling the call of the Mideast," she warned. Trace headed for the stairs. "Feeling kinda spanakopita, kinda tabbouleh, kinda baba ghanoushy, kinda . . ." Her voice trailed off. By the time Trace reached his room he could hear the doorbell ringing. Auntie Lea didn't cook every night, but when she did, her Cuties appeared right on time.

"Hello, Mrs. Lee. This is Trace Carter, is Ty home?"

"Hi, Trace. I think he's in his room. He must not have heard his phone; did you call his cell?" Tiberius's mom asked.

"Yes, ma'am. Maybe he's recharging it or . . ." He trailed off. Ty's mom had gone to call him, but Trace was the one getting the message: Ty didn't want to talk to him. This was stupid. They were supposed to be partners. While he waited, Trace slipped under the loft bed, sat at his desk, and kicked off his shoes.

"Whaddya want?" Ty said when he came to the phone. He sounded bored and annoyed, too busy for even a *hello*.

"What I want," Trace began, forcing himself to stay pleasant, "what I wanted was to check in with you and apologize for this afternoon." That was a lie. He had nothing to apologize for. This was stupid. "What happened was—"

"Look, just get your outline together for Tuesday. Presley said she would tell you what we did, so just get it together and bring copies for everyone, okay? Okay." Ty hung up.

Trace glared at the phone. Ty had *not* just hung up on him. No, it wasn't okay. What was his problem? If things had been reversed he would have assumed something had come up, at the very least he would hear Ty out, let him explain. Stretching his legs under the desk, he studied the blank wall before him. A row of faint rectangles reminded him that Auntie Lea had removed pictures so that he could hang his own on this wall. Not yet. Maybe not ever.

This day could not end soon enough.

Trace fired up his laptop to check the NYPL website. Good. The library had Sunday hours. He could go tomorrow, get his outline together, and at least *that* would be done. He should have asked Presley for details. Like what topics he had agreed to cover, for one thing. And maybe why Ty was so pissed. He should text her, call her. But Presley Jackson? Jackson was way too common a name. She said she lived nearby, but their neighborhood was probably crawling with Jacksons.

He would *not* be calling Ty again, that much he knew. And tracking down Kali was out of the question. There couldn't be too many Kali Castleberrys on Facebook, but even if he found her, the girl was not about to friend him.

Pulling a notepad out of his desk, he wrote *1860* in big numerals across the top. This is what he should do. Start on his outline. But all he recalled was that his topics sucked. The girls had grabbed the good stuff, like Jesse James and John Wilkes Booth. Trace groaned as Ty's words suddenly came back to him. He had been left with slavery, the KKK, and Jim Crow, who apparently was not even a real person. Great.

Trace closed his laptop and pushed back from his desk, bumping his head on the ladder. It was too early for bed, but the thought of climbing up and burying himself under the covers was tempting. Music from stringed instruments drifted into his room, followed by shouts of *opa! opa!* from downstairs. Dinner must be ready.

Trace padded down the stairs in his socks. His aunt and two other women were lined up, hands on one another's hips, swaying around the kitchen like a large, gangly caterpillar to music streaming from the speakers on top of the refrigerator.

"We are in for a treat tonight, my man," Auntie Lea said. Her cheeks were flushed and, considering how worried he had been about her feelings just hours ago, it felt good to see her smiling.

"This is Vesper; I think you guys met when you first got here." Trace nodded at the stocky Hispanic woman. He remembered the map of freckles covering her face but not much more. Auntie Lea was grabbing plates and glasses. "And this is her roommate, Talia," she said over her shoulder. "Sit, sit, sit, you guys."

Trace sat. Auntie Lea turned down the music and the Cuties dug in, chattering away. He didn't wait. There was hummus and pita bread, tabbouleh and lentil soup, followed by large, warm pillows of spanakopita. Trace had never been a fan of spinach before, but his aunt served these little turnovers often and he knew he liked them.

His mind wandered as Vesper rambled on and on about her latest project: a photographic family tree. She and Talia were both photographers or taught photography or had met on a photo shoot or they liked photography, or *something* about photography was involved. He wondered if the two women were roommates or girlfriends. Trace was not exactly sure what lesbians did with each other. Vesper looked mighty soft and chunky, but Talia was a tiny thing with sharp edges. Her chin was pointy, her shoulders looked pointy, even her ears came to Spock-like points. Whatever they did together probably left Vesper bruised. He grinned at the thought of them tangled around each other and nodded to himself. Live long and prosper, ladies.

"You like that idea, Theo?" Auntie Lea suddenly

said. "Okay, we'll do it." She smiled at him happily, as though he had been nodding at her. "All that stuff of Aunt Frenchy's? We'll start with that."

"Co-o-o-ol," Trace said slowly, returning her smile. Now what? He had to stop agreeing to stuff accidentally.

So now he listened. The women were talking about DNA traces that revealed where in the world your ancestors had come from. Auntie Lea eagerly pulled out one of Aunt Frenchy's photo albums and the Cuties began oohing and aahing over the cracked and faded images. Even from across the table and upside down he recognized a picture of his mom when she was about his age. No way was he going through those pictures.

Trace felt warm. It wasn't a good warm, though. They were passing around a plate piled with stuffed grape leaves and Trace leaned away, unable to hide a grimace as Vesper offered them to him. Cold rice and wet leaves? No. The damp and too-dark green clumps looked as if they'd been underwater for a long, long time. Trace pushed away from the table.

"Hey, wait," Auntie Lea pleaded. "Where's your sense of adventure? You have *got* to try the dessert

Talia brought." Pulling a round, undulating pastry out of a box, she set it before him. Its flaky surface glistened menacingly.

"Galactoboureko!" Talia breathed, her eyes all glittery.

So she really *was* a Vulcan.

The wide stone steps in front of the library were packed with people, but Trace found a space in the shadow of the lions and shrugged his book bag off his shoulders. The morning had been gray and chilly and now that the sun had come out, it felt nice just to sit and soak it in for a minute. Well, to sit and to check out the steady stream of girls walking down Fifth Avenue, clustered at the bus stop, and stretched out on the steps around him.

The sun was making him drowsy. It had been a rough night. He knew he must have had the dream again. But here, in the soothing daylight, he was glad he couldn't remember any details. His bed had been a mess when he woke up: sheets twisted into knots, blankets dropped to the floor, his pillow bunched up and cowering in a corner as though trying to escape. Whatever he had been running from in his sleep had chased him right into consciousness at the crack of dawn. Trace could not remember the last time he had been able to sleep late. He closed his eyes and leaned back on his elbows.

"So you saw the ghost, huh?" A man's voice in his ear made him jump.

"Wha . . . ?" A tall, brown-skinned man with a mustache had folded himself onto the step next to Trace.

"Whaddya mean? W . . . w . . . who are you?" Trace stammered. The air tightened around him and he suddenly saw, in great detail, the little closet of a room that Lemuel T. Spitz had held him in only yesterday. It was the guy who had come to take the broken chair and table from the guard's office.

The man just smiled, tilted his face to the sun, and leaned back on his elbows too. "Relax, kid," he finally said. "My name is Dallas Houston." He gave Trace a knowing look out of the corner of his eye and grinned as though he was waiting for a comeback. "Go ahead, say it. I know it's a messed-up name." When Trace said nothing, the man sat up and leaned toward him, nudging his arm as though they were old buddies.

"I've seen him too, you know," Dallas said quietly. "My workshop's down there. Woodworking, handy-man stuff—whatever needs fixing, I fix. I hear the kid from time to time. Even think I catch a glimpse of him once in a while. But I never get a *really* good look, you know?" Dallas Houston leaned back on the steps again, turning his face to the sky.

Trace said nothing, just glared at the street below. So he had *known* about the boy? Fifth Avenue was jumping: people walking by, getting on buses, sprint-ing through traffic. There were cars honking, tires screeching, chatter, even birdcalls if he listened hard enough. Everything looked clear, sharp-edged, solid and real.

"I only get a quick glimpse," Dallas was saying, "but he kinda fades away if I look right at him. Did he do that to you?"

Trace pressed his lips together tightly. *Now* the man wanted to talk?

Dallas nodded as though he already knew Trace's

answer. "Every now and again . . . can't put my finger on just *how* I know . . . but I know he's there. Something kinda electrical happens to the air. Did you get that?"

"What are you *talking* about?" Trace blurted out. But he knew. Because his skin was all prickly again, that weird tingling sensation was back. "What do you mean, '*fades* away'?" He realized he had spoken too harshly, given away too much.

"He's crying, right?" Dallas asked. "And raggedy?"

Trace slipped the straps of his backpack over his shoulders again and got up to leave. That raggedy kid was at the top of his list of things to *not* think about. With just a bit more time, the boy would become something imagined, a daydream, one of those shadows you catch moving from the corner of your eye. But when you look, it's just a chair out of position, or a lampshade hung crookedly, or an unfamiliar coat draped on a rack. It's not real. At least, it would not be if he kept working on it. The man tapped at his ankle.

"You're *not* crazy," Dallas Houston said. He was shielding his eyes against the sun as he looked up at Trace. "That boy's down there all right. For some reason, he let you get a good look at him."

The boy's face, his eyes wet in the glow of the red light, drifted into Trace's mind. The prickly, electrical sensation was fading, but now he felt uneasy, antsy, like there was something important he should be doing. What he felt like doing was kicking the man.

"If you knew he was there, why didn't you say something? Why didn't you tell that guard who was grilling me like I was a kidnapper or something? Why tell me now, *Dallas Houston*?" Trace sneered, trying to turn the man's name into a nasty punch line.

"No point. Those guards won't find him," Dallas said evenly. Beneath his hand, Dallas's shaded eyes locked onto Trace's. "He finds you. I think the kid's waiting for someone." The man paused, but Trace was already turning, heading up the steps.

"He's down there all right," Dallas called after him. "And he *is* a ghost."

Trace felt good about the information he had collected. It had taken him one hour and forty-five minutes in the Reading Room: one hour for research and forty-five minutes to get his heart to stop racing, his fingers to stop vibrating as he tried to make notes. He could not decide if having someone confirm that he had seen a ghost was a good thing or a totally mind-altering, earthshaking, bone-rattling thing. Ghosts were fine in Stephen King or Peter Straub books. He could handle them easily in the dark with a box of popcorn and some 3-D glasses. But not underneath the streets of midtown Manhattan on a trip to the public library.

He spread his notes across his loft bed and was staring out the window below at the remains of Auntie Lea's herb garden and flower beds. They were bathed in that last blast of pink light before the day slid into darkness. But it was a phony pink. A cold pink. Nothing warm about it. Winter was coming. A sudden image of his mom, her face made up to be artificially rosy at the funeral, came to mind and made him wince, stabbed him somewhere in his chest.

He pushed it back. Think about other things. Push it back. This, Trace realized, was becoming his talent: he could stop thoughts. He just needed other thoughts to knock them off center stage. So he studied the notes he had made in the Reading Room. The three pages he had filled with notes on the Ku Klux Klan were enough to let him know he would have never survived "back in the day." No way would he have been able to put up with being taunted and harassed, treated like a criminal. Trace slammed his notebook closed. Well, maybe things had not changed so very much. New faces, new methods. Same crap.

In one sweep, Trace pushed papers, notebook, and pens off the bed, enjoying the slapping sounds as everything hit the floor below. Falling backward onto his pillow, he planted his feet on the ceiling. There was a hole in one sock, almost large enough for him to poke his big toe through. Only last week it had been just a little pinhole. This was how everything went. Everything came apart, ripped and unraveled, crumbled and died. And who was going to tell him to toss these socks out now or take him to get new ones? Who even noticed if he changed them or washed them or even *wore* them? No one. Not anymore. It was all on him now.

Something poked at his hip, and, rolling slightly, he fished underneath him and pulled out a little orange card that must have fallen from between his papers.

**DALLAS HOUSTON**
**Carpentry ~ Restoration ~ Fine Woodwork.**
**goodasnew@dhouston.com**
**212.555.1303**

"Seriously?" Trace asked aloud. He folded the card, as best he could, into a tiny paper plane and sent it flying. It bounced off the windowpane before landing somewhere down below. What did the guy think, that he wanted to go on a ghost hunt? Now that was just creepy.

# 10

Ty had managed to duck him most of the day, and by lunchtime, Trace had decided he could not care less. He was studying the food on his plate, wondering what it had been in a previous life, when Presley slid her tray onto the table and plopped down opposite him, already midstream in a conversation she seemed to think they were having.

". . . like she was ready to annihilate us, like totally eviscerate Ty *and* me, you know?" Presley looked up at Trace, disbelief and dots of tomato sauce on her face. "Her patience level is very, I mean VERY minuscule, abbreviated, like . . . like, *epigrammatic*, know what I mean?" Trace didn't. Presley wiped her face, shook her head, and began furiously trying to cut whatever lay under the spaghetti sauce.

"So . . . ," Trace ventured. "Ty's angry at me because Kali got pissed?"

Presley sputtered. She took a sip of water, put down her knife and fork, and leaned across the table, checking over her shoulders as though Kali might be near. "Pissed is for humans; she went total alien cyborg ninja on us. Good thing there were guards."

Trace grunted. Another day, they might have an interesting debate on whether or not guards were a "good thing." But he was thinking about his friend. If Ty had felt hurt just because Trace skipped over him and chose Kali first, he probably still had scar tissue after she had publicly blasted him like that. Why was she so upset? Maybe she really did like him? Like how little kids threw things at the one they really liked? Maybe she had been hoping they would get together?

"So just give him time, 'cause he's sensitive, you know?" Presley concluded. She had been steadily talking and now Trace tuned back in. Stabbing a dainty forkful of cake that was slathered in Day-Glo–orange frosting, Presley pointed it meaningfully at

Trace. "Ty needs an intermission. A hiatus. A *lacuna*. You know? Time."

Then she turned on a dime and began burbling happily about little-known Abraham Lincoln factoids she had uncovered on Lincoln's cat, his hat, his favorite dessert. Trace pretended to focus on what remained of his salad and tuned back out.

Time. The first time Trace had met with Dr. Proctor, that had been all she seemed to want to talk about too. "Ever given much thought to time?" she had asked. He remembered sneaking a glance at the clock behind the doctor's head. His only thought about time was about how much of it he had to spend in that office, how soon he could leave.

"If there really were time machines, if you really could set a dial and pick a time, if you *could* go back, to that evening on the highway, to the night of the accident, could you have done anything differently?" Dr. Proctor leaned back in her chair, a gentle, quizzical smile on her face, as though she really did hope he would take her back to that bridge, back to the river.

"W . . . what are you . . ." Trace had gulped. She had trapped him that quickly. "What do you *mean*, do differently?" Did she know it was his fault? That he was the only one who might have changed things? Even now, in the cafeteria, with Presley chattering about cakes and cats and assassinations, he could feel that horrible sensation of his throat tightening, the water pressing.

"It's just a hypothetical question," the doctor had said, "a what-if?"

"I . . . I wouldn't be there. I m-mean, *we*. We wouldn't be there," Trace had stammered. "If I went back, I would . . . I would . . ." The dank smell of the river had seeped into the doctor's room, sweating its way out of the stripes in the wallpaper. He had felt light-headed. Certain that if he didn't leave, he really would find himself back there, be somehow delivered to that shore *again*, facing that water *again*. He would stand waiting as the car was wrenched out of the river, *again*, water crying out of every seam.

The bell rang. Trace looked up to see Presley dabbing at a splotch of orange Day-Glo frosting that had become imbedded in her navy-blue sweater. Flashing a quick smile, she scooped up her tray and headed into the flow of students leaving the cafeteria.

Trace made it to English Lit with only seconds to spare. He had finished reading the Shakespeare assignment, but the language had been a pain to follow. He dreaded the hunt for metaphors and symbols that Mrs. Madden would swear were in there. But the teacher flipped off the lights and suddenly an old black-and-white movie flickered across the large screen at the front of the class: *A Midsummer Night's Dream*. They had made this thing into a movie? Trace watched as smoky white mist streamed through a dark forest, swirling gently as fairies emerged from it. The old-timey special effects made everything look glittery and soft. Mrs. Madden had said the movie was made in 1935, nearly eighty-five years ago. So all those fairies, even the young boy playing Puck, were probably dead now. But still they danced through those dark woods, trapped in time, all shimmering ghosts. Time could save only their images.

If he could travel through time, he wouldn't go back and see dinosaurs like everyone did in sci-fi movies. Or to Egypt to find out how they really built the pyramids. He wouldn't zing ahead either. Trace closed his eyes in the darkened room. He would never travel to a time when everyone he knew was just a memory captured on film. No. He knew he would go back to that day. To a few hours before the accident.

✳✳✳

The halls emptied quickly after the last bell and Trace found he had them to himself as he headed for the media center. Time really did make a difference: those halls had been packed that morning. He had walked through them like the invisible man, passing the same kids who ignored him seven hours a day, five days a week. But it was impossible *not* to brush into them, *not* to catch bits of conversation, *not* to get a whiff of their soap, hair oil, perfume, funk. Tomorrow morning, the noise level would be deafening. But now only the sound of his own footsteps bounced off the walls and lockers. Whether crowded or empty, Trace thought, in those halls he was invisible.

Ms. Levy, the librarian, was on the phone when he entered the media center. She nodded, smiled, and pointed at the clock that hung above a row of shelves behind her. Trace knew she was about to close, but he wanted to arm himself with a few more notes before meeting with the study group tomorrow. This time, he would not be late, he would not be unprepared, and he would not just bring in what was expected. The 1860s were a gold mine, and he was going to dig up some nuggets that would impress even Kali.

"Draft riots and the KKK," Ms. Levy said, swiping

the bar codes of the books Trace had quickly chosen. "This is Mrs. Weaver's class?" The librarian handed him the books with a knowing grin. "The twenties, fifties, and seventies *still* haven't been in here," she said pointedly. "You'd best tell your classmates to get busy. Practically all of the 1800s has been checked out."

Trace smiled. "Will do," he lied. He liked Ms. Levy.

She was not anything like what he always thought librarians were supposed to be. She was a curvy, latte-colored Dominican with a Jewish name, an adult who looked like more like a teenager, and she was too chatty to shush anyone without starting up a long conversation. She wore stilettos and leather jackets and she had a tattoo on her back. He had only seen it once. Well, part of it: the head of some kind of bird that was only visible because the sweater she wore one day scooped low on her back. That tattoo was the object of much speculation, Trace knew. Guys in his class talked *about* her, crudely assessed her looks, her body, and how they could make that bird of hers sing, talk, holler. But they didn't talk *to* her, Trace noticed. The guys who wolfed the loudest barely spoke a word to her whenever she checked out their books or helped them on the computer. And when they did manage to mumble something, they sounded like first graders squeaking out a "Thank you" or a "Yes, Ms. Levy."

But Ms. Levy reminded him of Auntie Lea a bit, and Trace thought that was why he felt comfortable with her from the first time he met her. She had put on her jacket, grabbed her huge purse, and was still talking as she pulled a ring of keys out of the top drawer of her desk.

"Wait up, Theo, I'll walk you out," she said. "The 1860s were pretty dynamic; you got the best decade." She smiled at Trace as though he had cleverly beat out the competition. "That's a great project that Mrs. Weaver does. Every year, someone digs up something that is news to me." Trace waited as she flipped off the lights and locked the door. "And I'm a real history buff, so that's saying something," Ms. Levy added.

"Anything you can tell me about the 1860s that might be surprising?" Trace asked as they headed for the front door. "I don't want to come in with the same ol', same ol' if I can help it." Anyone seeing them might think they were just two friends, Trace thought, walking along after class talking about an assignment.

"Well, that book you picked on the draft riots should be interesting," the librarian said as they left the school. "You know about the fire at the Colored Orphan Asylum?"

Trace shook his head and grimaced. "Colored?"

Ms. Levy laughed. "Yes, young man. Back in the day, we wuz 'colored,'" she said, sounding very street. Shoving a hand into her large purse, she pulled out a shiny, dark-blue motorcycle helmet. She raised one eyebrow in response to Trace's surprised look, then walked over to a motorcycle parked at the curb and rested her bag in a compartment behind the seat.

"It was one of the worst fires on record in the city," Ms. Levy said. "Rioters burned the Orphan Asylum down. Gangs of hooligans mostly. Misplaced anger, I'd call it. Because they blamed black folks for Lincoln's Draft Act in 1863." Ms. Levy climbed onto the bike and rested the helmet in her lap. "Most accounts say the children in the orphanage were all taken to safety. But dig around, Theo. Once or twice I've come across a report that says one child *was* killed, and I'd like to know what you find out, okay?" Pulling gloves from her jacket pockets, she snapped them onto her hands.

"Whoa," Trace said, shaking his head. "So you're like a librarian road warrior?"

Ms. Levy just tugged her helmet over her head,

lifting the Plexiglas face guard to roll her eyes at him.

Trace held up the books he had checked out. "Will do, Ms. Levy. The Colored Orphan Asylum fire, 1863. One child possibly killed. I'm all over it. Where was the orphanage, anyway?"

"Hey, this is *your* report, do your research," the librarian scoffed. Starting her motorcycle, she brushed away the kickstand with her foot. Just before she flipped the visor down, though, she gave Trace a look of mock pity.

"Okay, okay. One tidbit: it was in the very heart of Manhattan. And they put a brand-new building up right over the ashes. Wild, right? It's the New York Public Library."

**11**

He had no idea how long he had been standing there,
rooted to the pavement. Rooted. How was it possible
that some phrases that he had heard all his life could
just suddenly snap into focus like this? He was rooted.
He had watched Ms. Levy pull off into traffic, people
had walked by him, there was a chilly wind kicking
up, and he really did not like the feel of the cold air.
But he was as unable to walk as if his feet had been
encased in cement. The library?

He saw again the dark-red light on the little boy's
face and all those dusty books on the shelf that he was
sure he had seen *right through* the threadbare shirt
that the boy wore. Trace felt queasy. Instinctively

dropping to one knee, he pretended to tie his shoelace. Once down on the ground, his head cleared a bit. He stayed like that as people rushed around him toward the subway, eager to get underground and away from the rising wind. When Trace finally did stand up, it was only the wind that unstuck him. Sometimes in his dreams, when he was standing on the riverbank, his legs felt leaden like this, numb. But at least he was able to move now. The wind bit into his ears and Trace turned his collar up against it, blocking it, trying to stifle it. *One child.*

The sudden warmth of the hallway brought on an unpleasant prickling sensation in his face and hands that woke him up. Trace had no memory of his trip home. He hung his jacket over a hook by the front door as the tiny needles attacking his fingertips began to calm down. One minute he had been watching Ms. Levy ride off on her bike, and now . . .

"We're in here!" Auntie Lea called out unnecessarily. Salsa music, voices, and the sound of running water were flowing toward him from the kitchen. A thin haze of smoke hanging like gauze beneath the hallway ceiling carried a promising aroma: it was

Mexican night. But as hungry as he was, Trace just wanted to duck up the stairs, drop his book bag, and lock himself in for the night. He would explain later, apologize later.

He was on the first step when a sudden clatter of silverware hitting the floor and a stream of high-pitched giggles stopped him. Those were girl giggles.

"Hola, señor-r-r-r," Auntie Lea said, rolling her *r*'s with some difficulty. "*¿Tienes hambr-r-r-re?*" She was wearing a colorful, flowing skirt, a blousy white top that bared her shoulders, and what had to be every string of beads from her worktable upstairs. A silk flower trapped in her hair had seen better days.

At the table, a short, stocky man with a mass of shiny hair was chopping onions. And crouched near his side, scooping up forks and knives into an apron that was way too long for her, was the giggler. She looked up at Trace and he had to smile.

"Theo, I'd like you to meet—" Auntie Lea began. But Trace had already dropped his book bag and crossed the kitchen to pick up the remaining knives. He gallantly offered his hand to help the girl up.

"Trace," he said, "Trace Carter." It came out like a flimsy version of "Bond, James Bond," and he immediately turned toward the man before the girl might catch him blushing. "Hello, sir," he said, shaking his hand.

The man grinned. "Roman," he said. "Roman Cervantes." His dark eyes crinkled with amusement, but if his intent was to mimic the Bond introduction, Trace found he didn't mind.

"And this is my Angélica," Roman said, reaching out to hug his daughter near to him.

"Just Angel, Papi," the girl said. "Hi, Trace. Hope you don't mind the home invasion. Papi said we were just 'stopping by' . . . like two hours ago." She laughed. Trace only managed a weak smile as he mumbled something that sounded like a cat caught in a couch cushion. She really *was* an angel. Clearing his throat, he looked away from her face again. "Anything I can do to help, Auntie Lea?" he asked.

His aunt turned toward him, hands on hips, head cocked to one side. More than a few dots of tomato sauce decorated the front of her otherwise snowy-white blouse.

"You look like you've been through the wringer, mister. Just get washed up. We've got this covered.

*Diner-r-r-r-ro* is in five minutes." Roman winced. Angel giggled.

Trace grabbed his book bag and raced up the stairs. *Money* in five minutes. That was more than enough time.

Over a dinner of guacamole and chips, cheese enchiladas, rice, refried beans, and Roman's "Saint Margaritas" (lemonade with seltzer, it turned out), Trace learned that their dinner guest was the Roman of Roman's Hardware on Myrtle Avenue and that he and Angel lived a million miles away in the Bronx. It had taken Trace only four minutes to wash up, change into his buttery yellow shirt, and swap his sneakers for a pair of loafers. He was finding it hard to look in Angel's direction and even harder *not* to.

"So I was in Roman's store, trying to find a screw for that leg on my bed, you know the one, Theo?" Auntie Lea was happily scooping rice onto her plate. "The creaking is making me crazy, I swear." She attacked the beans next.

"A couple of avocados rolled outa her shopping bag onto the counter," Roman continued. "So what could I do?" He laughed heartily as Auntie Lea nodded and Angel rolled her eyes.

"I'm not . . . I don't . . . ?" Trace said. He didn't get it.

Angel reached across the table and put her hand on his arm reassuringly. "Dad's, like, the guacamole king," she said lightly. "He's never met an avocado he didn't want to pulverize into dip." Trace felt his face flush again at her sudden touch, but, to his relief, the girl didn't seem to notice.

"Well, he began telling me how to make a mean bowl o' guac but, hey, if I have the master standing right there, for cryin' out loud, what could I do but invite him to dinner?" Auntie Lea said, popping a chip loaded with guacamole into her mouth.

"We're full-service at Roman's Hardware. Nuts, bolts, and so much more." Roman beamed.

"You should see the place, Theo," his aunt said. "Roman's got this shelf that runs all the way around the store, maybe six feet up, and he's got a collection of metal *everything*. All this stuff: radios, buttons, old tin cans with cool advertising on them, whirligigs, thingamabobs, all kinda metal toys. It's surreal."

"Or what my mom used to call *junk*," Angel chimed

in. Roman made a wounded face at her. "Please, Papi, you *know* you only put that shelf up 'cause Mami made you get all that mess outa the apartment."

Auntie Lea hopped up from the table, and as Roman began to stand up, she motioned for him to stay put. *Old school*, Trace thought. But he wondered if maybe he should have stood up too. Maybe Angel was used to those sorts of manners. Maybe she thought he was rude. But Angel was concentrating on pouring herself another glassful of Saint Margarita.

"That mess, as you call it, is good stuff," Roman grumbled. "Some of those pieces are valuable antiques, young lady. Fact is, that 'junk' might just put you through college. That is, if you don't get so smart you don't need to go."

Angel raised an eyebrow at her dad. Trace could tell they bantered like this all the time, and it made him wonder about where her mom was. Then she turned and gave him a conspiratorial wink. Now he had to wonder about *that*.

Just then, Auntie Lea reappeared, cupping something in her hands. She sat down and slid the metal toy from Aunt Frenchy's basket across the table to Roman.

"Any idea what this is?" she asked.

Roman carefully wiped his lips with a napkin, reached into his shirt pocket, and pulled out a rimless pair of glasses. "Definitely a toy," he began. "Could be as early as the Civil War? Not sure about the time, but they were making tin toys like this as far back as the 1840s, maybe even earlier." Roman rolled the toy around in his hands. "It's some kind of rattle; that you'd already know. Probably for a toddler since it has the ABCs all over it. And probably not from a very well-to-do family since it looks crudely made, even for the time." He ran his thumb over the letters hammered into the side of the rattle, then shook it a few times and laid it on the table.

"Where'd you get it?" he asked.

Auntie Lea pushed back from the table, waving again at Roman to stay seated as she started to collect plates. "It was in a bunch of old stuff my mom gave me from an aunt who died recently. It was the only thing like that in the pile, though. That old, I mean. Or a toy."

Trace could feel Auntie Lea watching him, but he kept his eyes on the cold beans and rice on his plate. The toy bothered him. More than bothered, it was making him think of that kid again. Angel had picked up the rattle and was shaking it. The noise grated on his nerves.

"Oh, sorry for your loss," Roman said. "Were you close?"

Angel was turning the rattle over again and again, pausing only to run her fingers over the alphabet like her dad had done. Trace knew it would seem insane for him to just grab it and make her stop.

"You finished?" Auntie Lea asked, reaching for his plate. Trace nodded. Angel really needed to put down the toy.

To Roman his aunt replied, "Not really. I mean, I didn't see her very often. But she didn't have children and I was her only niece. Our family's been all girls since, well, since forever I guess. Until this guy here." Auntie Lea nodded toward Trace, then turned to open a bakery box that had been sitting on the stove.

"Flan de ca*rrrrrrr*amelo, anyone?" she asked with a wicked grin.

It was midnight. Trace had escaped to his room, citing tons of homework as his reason to skip dessert. He actually did have a lot to do. He needed back-to-back, mind-boggling facts to throw on the table when the group met tomorrow. But instead of cracking open the books he had brought home, he had been lying in bed, dozing and waking, his feet on and off the ceiling for hours.

And rather than untangling the threads he felt snarling up his mind, he was trying to focus on Angel. When she had looked up at him the first time, what kind of look had that been on her face? And then when she put her hand on his arm, what was *that* about? Trace was pretty sure she was older than he was, but not by much. So how old *was* she? Maybe fifteen? She was really pretty. Not the same pretty as Kali, who was a kind of exotic, fashion-model, high-cheekbones, snooty sort of pretty. Angel was more like the sweet sort of pretty, the kind of girl who was friendly to everyone and who might like a guy even if he was younger. It was not working. Thinking about her just made things seem *more* muddled. He needed to sleep.

"Okay," he said aloud, the sound of his own voice spooking him in the dark. His words were, in fact, so disembodied that, with very little effort, he could believe someone else had spoken. Trace needed to shake off whatever it was that was making him feel so edgy. He would get up early and do enough research to be ready for the meeting. He would pull it together. Presley was in his corner, but Ty and Kali? They would be so impressed they would *have* to come around. He would make things right.

"Okay," he repeated sleepily. "KKK. Jim Crow. Draft riots. First thing tomorrow." Trace turned onto his stomach, flipped his pillow over, and, wrapping his arms around it, sunk his cheek into its cool softness. *Everything would be fine. 1860s. That was what? Like over a hundred and fifty years . . . ages and ages ago? Ages and ages . . .* Angel's face smiled up at him. "Ages, Papi," she whispered. *They burned an orphanage,* Trace tried to tell her. "Harsh." Angel sighed. *Who would do that, right? Little kids. Fire. Man, that's sad.* "I know. I know." Angel was shaking her head slowly. It kind of rattled when she did that and Trace frowned into the pillow. Should he tell her about the library being built over ashes? Or the one kid who was, well, was *possibly . . . No. No, Angel, not that kid. Not my kid. That little guy was just . . .* Trace breathed into the pillow. *He was lost, probably. Just lost.* He wanted to reassure Angel, but she was drifting away. Smiling, drifting, shaking her head. Trace held out his hand, trying to pull her back. *Take my hand*. He almost . . . almost had her hand . . . Slowly, slowly, Angel's face turned toward him. Her soft eyes were filling with water. Trace choked. That same sick, green water. He was in the river.

# 12

It was probably the dream that had made him bolt awake at 5:26 a.m., but Trace had wanted to get up early anyway. So, there *was* a silver lining to his dark cloud. Judging by the low snores and occasional creaks from Auntie Lea's room, he was on his own for breakfast. With the kitchen to himself, he had been able to listen to some Jay-Z, surf the internet, take notes, and stuff himself with oatmeal without interruption.

He was feeling pretty good as he left the apartment. He threaded his way along streets filled with children on their way to school, all twitchy in anticipation of Halloween, which was four whole days away. Had he ever been that excited about trick-or-treating when he was little? Trace tried to remember back to when he was a kid. Back *before*. Sometimes, it seemed to Trace as if a heavy curtain, like the thick red velvet kind that hung in old-time movie theaters, had dropped over his past. Onstage in front was everything that happened *after* the accident. But everything *before* was back there behind the curtain. Trapped like a moth in a glass, its frantic beating of wings muffled. At least, he thought it was all there. He felt sure he could look behind the curtain and remember everything, anything— if ever he wanted to. But not today. Today, he needed to feel good.

A frothy pink tutu peeked out of a little girl's down jacket as she skipped past him, holding her mother's hand. And ahead at the corner, a tiny boy with a pair of bumblebee antennae balanced crookedly atop his hoodie bounced as he waited for the light to change. All along the street, witches and the occasional skull leered out from store windows.

How did it work here? Back in Baltimore, kids could knock on doors at real houses with lawns and garages. But here in Brooklyn, did they have to trek up and down the high stoops of brownstones or take elevators to apartment hallways lined with strangers' doors?

They *must*, he thought. Cobwebs and jack-o'-lanterns decorated many of the railings and doorsteps along his path to the subway. The trick-or-treating must go on.

When he reached the front steps at IS 99, Trace found them deserted. He took that as a good sign, although it was cold weather and not, he suspected, the gods of good fortune he should thank. Any unscheduled run-ins with Kali or Ty might mess up his plan for their study group meeting after class. School was letting out early for a teachers' meeting: sign number two that this might just be a perfect day. Soon, everything would be put right. After all, he was the one who had been chosen team leader. Today, Ty and Kali would see the cool, calm, confident style that would make their team the one to beat. Today, things would change.

"What'd you find out, Theo?" Ms. Levy whispered loudly as Trace entered the media center. With one arm loaded with books and a coffee cup in her other hand, she was using her hip to nudge along a cart that held a computer and a projector. Ms. Levy was an accident waiting to happen. Clusters of students, some study-ing, others bent over cell phones, filled the library.

"Let me take those," Trace offered, relieving the librarian of both the books and her coffee cup. A group of girls near the photocopier on the far side of the room began arguing loudly. A shout erupted from a pair of guys waging battle in a game on their phones. *Quiet Zone* signs, placed strategically around the library, were covered with comments and provocative drawings, although Ms. Levy refreshed them daily and it was barely noon.

"About the Colored Orphan Asylum fire, I mean?" the librarian asked, still whispering. Parking the cart, she took her coffee cup back and cleared a spot on her desk for the books.

Trace smiled. "Nothing definite, Ms. Levy," he answered quietly. "I did see what you were talking about, though. There are some stories about a nine-year-old girl being killed, but not by the fire. The crowd beat her to death."

The anguish on Ms. Levy's face made Trace instantly regret that he had rolled off the information so casually. He had actually been relieved to read that it was a nine-year-old girl and not a four-year-old boy who had died. Suddenly realizing how twisted that thought was, he flushed with embarrassment.

"I . . . I thought you already knew that . . . when you told me about a child . . . ," Trace began.

"No," Ms. Levy said softly. "That's awful." She sat at her desk looking up at him. "I remember seeing some reference to a child being killed during the riot, but I didn't see any details. That's horrible. That's . . ." She trailed off.

"There were only a couple of references about it, Ms. Levy. Most of the sites and those books I took out don't mention a girl at all," Trace offered. He glanced at the clock, then took a quick look around, satisfying himself that the others had not arrived. His plan had been to come early, spread his notes over the table near the copier, and impress the others. But the arguing girls seemed to be on the verge of throwing punches, so he decided that using a different table near the window would be just fine.

"No worries, Theo," Ms. Levy said. "It was a long time ago, poor thing." Giving him a sad smile, she took a sip of her coffee. "But let me know if you do find out anything more about the girl, okay?"

Trace nodded. As he turned to set up at the window table, he nearly stepped on Kali. She stopped short, sniffed, and headed for the table closest to the copier.

The noisy fussing over who was taking too long, what the limit should be on the number of pages copied at one time, and who had *really* gotten there first suddenly stopped. Kali spoke to the girls so quietly that Trace, only steps away, heard nothing. But the girls suddenly packed up their books, papers, and purses and hurried to a table across the room.

He watched Kali carefully arrange four color-coded sets of index cards in rows before her, take out a notebook and pen, and flip open an iPad. So much for impressing everyone with *his* organization, Trace thought, quietly pulling out his books and sliding into the seat opposite her. The scrawled pages in his notebook seemed amateurish now. He should have thought of index cards. Ty and Presley arrived just as he sat down.

"As a thespian myself," Presley was saying, "I just can't fathom how innervated Mrs. Lincoln must have been, you know? Like she goes out to be titillated by an evening of regalement and divertissement and then, BLAM! there's all that consternation and her husband is, like, totally extirpated right in front of her, splattering gore and viscera all over the—"

"Shhhhhhhh!" Ty hissed. "This is a library, you

know. We're supposed to keep it down, Presley." He rolled his eyes at Trace and for a second, Trace thought things might be back to normal. But no. Ty took a seat at the side of the table and pulled out a notebook, index cards, and a pen. "Hey, Kali, nice to see you're so prepared," he said, pointedly *not* speaking to Trace.

"Let's just do this, Tiberius," said Kali wearily. "We'll have fifteen minutes for our presentation, so I figure we should plan on three minutes each. With three or four topics apiece, that's not much, but we're supposed to leave time for Q and A."

"Want me to make a poster board for all of us?" Presley asked. She upturned her book bag next to Trace's notebook on the table, spilling forth Post-it notes, a Day-Glo highlighter, magazine clippings, one pencil box and sharpener, two MetroCards, a tattered sketchbook, lip gloss, her dog-eared copy of *Word Power Made Easy*, and what appeared to be a partially eaten granola bar. "I've already started mine 'cause I found this *really* cool picture of John Wilkes Booth on an old Wanted poster and you know what they say—"

Kali leveled a withering look her way, but Presley, busily picking pencil shavings off the granola bar, missed it.

"A picture's worth a thousand words," she chirped. "Which is kinda weird because a thousand's like five pages of words . . . and what point size is that anyway? . . . unless you don't double-space, which I think we're supposed to do unless—"

"Shut *up*, Presley!" Kali hissed. "We don't need your endless chatter. Good grief. Everybody else will have nearly five minutes apiece, but Mrs. Weaver had to go and stick you on our team, so we're already limited. The very *least* you can do is keep your ranting down while we're trying to work, okay?" Kali waved a hand around her head like she was warding off mosquitoes and then started itemizing the three topics she had decided to cover.

Trace watched the air go right out of Presley, and now she sat staring at her pile of stuff as if it had crawled up onto the table by itself and done something awful and rude and embarrassing.

"Look, Kali," he said firmly.

Kali paused. Ty looked up expectantly.

It was time for him to act like the team leader. "We're a team and we need to work like one. So the *first* thing you need to do is to apologize to Presley." Kali turned toward him, eyes narrowed, clearly ready to fire. But, having started, Trace realized that he actually had a whole list of things to tell Kali she needed to do. How could he have possibly thought that she had been looking forward to seeing him at the library? She had just been furious about him wasting her precious time. Furious and mean. So she had taken her anger out on Ty and Presley.

"I don't need *you* sticking up for me!" Presley suddenly snapped, her face turning a hot pink. She began shoving the mess on the table back into her bag.

"Huh?" Trace jerked back in his seat, confused. Ty frowned and even Kali looked surprised. "What did *I* do?"

Presley's chair screeched as she pushed it back. Yanking her book bag onto her shoulder, she scraped granola crumbs off the table into her palm and then glared at Trace. "I did a lot of work. I know you guys don't want me on the team, but you're not even speaking to one another, so I try to be nice to all of you so we at least can communicate. But we're *not* friends. I get it. And I'm *not* ranting!"

"Geeeeeeeeesh," Kali muttered under her breath.

"Shut UP," Trace barked at her.

"You, too," Presley continued, looking at Trace with

such hurt that he felt a crushing guilt. But for what he did not know.

"What did *I* do?" he said softly.

"You pretend we're friends and we have hot chocolate and cookies and everything and I meet your aunt and you're all nice and we're gonna work together and then you just walk right past me and don't even say hi when I speak to you, like you don't know me outside of school and—"

"Wai . . . wait a minute," Trace said. "I do too speak to you, what are you talking about? When don't I speak to you?" Now he felt impatient. This was his day to set things right, and now this? Presley was the only one he had *not* been worried about. Girls were a trip.

"I'll have my end of the report done, don't worry. But I don't need to work with her," Presley said, sticking her chin out at Kali. "Ty, you're okay, I guess," she added. Ty smiled weakly.

"But you? You walked right past me yesterday on Myrtle," Presley said now to Trace. "Don't act like you didn't see me. I was at the vegetable stand right on the corner of Vanderbilt and I even spoke to you and you guys just sailed by me like I wasn't even there."

"Wha . . . ? I got home late, Presley, and it was

kinda dark. Maybe you saw someone who looks like me, but I swear, I didn't see you." It was true that the walk home yesterday evening had been a blur. His mind had been stuck in 1863—up under the New York Public Library. But enough of this. Trace felt uneasy. It was time to get back to the report, time for him to be team leader, and time for Ty and Kali to drop the attitudes. He watched Presley zip up her jacket, spilling the granola crumbs down the front as she did. Fine. So maybe his team would be short one member for today. Presley would calm down. This had to be some kind of girl thing.

Trace watched as she wound a scarf around her chin. "It *was* you," she said hotly, staring him in the eye. "You were with a wild-haired little kid in a creepy rag costume."

Trace turned to ice.

"Oh—and if you take him out on Halloween like that," she added, "make him wear *real* shoes, you jerk."

Trace's mind went blank. And by the time he could think again, Presley had left the building.

The cold air helped. Trace walked along Clinton Avenue, keeping an eye on everyone he passed. He was trying hard to pay attention. Because he knew he had not seen Presley, not even heard her. Maybe she was mistaken. Maybe there really was someone who looked a lot like him. Someone who was with a kid who was dressed like . . . like . . . Well, it was just stupid. There had been a few kids in costumes on the streets last night. What was the deal with people in Brooklyn? Why the dress rehearsal? Couldn't parents make their kids wait until it was really Halloween? Presley had just gotten confused. Probably.

She *probably* had just had her feelings hurt. She *probably* wanted to snap at Kali for embarrassing her but had taken it out on him instead. It didn't have to make sense. The way she babbled, Presley *probably* got her feelings hurt on an hourly basis. There were a lot of *probably*s.

More than once as he walked, Trace jumped at the sound of footsteps behind him, making his heart race. More than once, he looked behind him, afraid he would see that boy. It was early afternoon and the sun was shining. But everything felt somehow unreal. That sun was *too* bright. Glaringly red maple and neon-yellow oak leaves fluttered against a sky that looked a bit *too* blue. Emerald-green hedges glistened behind jet-black railings, deep-orange pumpkins lined steps that all seemed to be the exact same shade of gray . . . Trace closed his eyes. The colors seemed exaggerated. It was as if they were trying to exactly match the ones in a box of Crayolas. Trace felt his head spinning. How could he ever know what was real? Could he really trust his own eyes? Looking down, he realized that even his own sneakers looked exactly like sneakers in a magazine ad: glossy, perfectly tied, and practically outlined against the sidewalk. Like the special effects in that movie they had watched, *A Midsummer Night's Dream*. Everything now looked glittery and shiny and . . . fake. The world was trying too hard to look real.

"Theo, my good sir!" a voice called out.

Trace spun around. He had reached Myrtle Avenue. From beneath the dark-green awning of his store window, Roman Cervantes was waving to him.

"Come, come," Roman called out.

Trace blinked and the otherworldly sensation began to melt. Blowing on his hands to warm them, he stumbled into Roman's Hardware. He was greeted by rows of wooden shelves stacked with a patchwork of boxes; a wall of drawers, some open and overflowing with spools of twine or string; and tall bins crammed with rolls of patterned paper, rods, and dowels. The air blanketing the store was warm and golden and soft and Trace instantly felt relieved.

As Angélica had promised, a shelf running high along the walls displayed her father's metal collection. Trace looked around, hoping she was there. Hadn't he dreamed about her last night?

"Do me a favor," Roman said, breaking into Trace's thoughts. With a long stick that ended in a pincer, the man airlifted an object from the overhead shelf and handed it to Trace. "Will you give this to your lovely aunt and tell her thanks for dinner?"

Trace studied the little metal box he had been handed.

"Angel and I usually just have takeout for dinner now that her mom's gone," Roman continued. "Last night reminded me how nice it felt to cook and sit down to a real meal." The man beamed, clearly remembering happier times.

What do you say at times like this? Trace wondered. He really wanted to know when and *how* Mrs.

Cervantes had died. She couldn't have been that old. But he was pretty sure it would be rude to ask. He turned the box over in his hands. Something was inside it. Trace resisted an urge to pop open the lid. That, too, might be rude, since it was meant for Auntie Lea.

So, maybe Angel was older, and maybe she lived all the way in the Bronx, but maybe they had more in common than she realized. Was it possible that losing one parent felt as painful as losing both? He should find out when she would be in the store again, when they might come over again. It was cool the way she and her dad were so close. He smiled to himself.

"Thanks, Mr. Cervantes," Trace said. "I'll give it to her.

"Whoa! Lose the *Mister*, son. *Mr.* Cervantes is my dad, okay? Just call me Roman—everyone else does." Grinning like the Cheshire cat, Roman put a hand on Trace's shoulder and steered him toward the door.

Trace felt he had to say something. It was weird to just let it hang in the air and not say *anything*. "I . . . I'm sorry for your loss, Roman. Yours and Angel's, I mean. Your . . . your wife. Sorry that she's—" Trace found he couldn't bring himself to say the word.

"Dead?" Roman burst out laughing. "Thanks, Theo, but she lives on West Eighty-Third . . . with her boyfriend."

Trace shoved the box into his pocket and yanked open the door. So much for trying to be polite. Even after the door had closed behind him and he had reached the corner, he was pretty sure he could still hear Roman's laughter.

# 13

Coming home to a kitchen filled with guests for dinner was normal. But it was the middle of the day and, somehow, Trace had expected silence, that he would have the place to himself. He really wanted to regroup and figure out a plan B.

But the nanosecond he opened the door he heard his aunt sing out, "Perfecto! Get in here *subito*, *signore*!" over the opera music that was playing in the kitchen. No psychic abilities were needed to guess that Auntie's Lea's Italian 101 phrases could only mean they were having pasta for dinner.

Trace was surprised to see that nothing was on the stove. A massive piece of white oaktag leaned against the wall of shelves in the kitchen where his aunt kept her collection of unopened cookbooks. On matching stools before it sat Auntie Lea and her friend Vesper. The kitchen table at their back was covered with photo albums and the basket of dusty stuff that had once belonged to Aunt Frenchy.

"Hey, Theo," Vesper said. "Aren't you home early?"

"Teachers' meeting," he answered absently, studying the board. A dozen Post-it notes were stuck on it in a pattern that resembled a pyramid; each bore a name and a set of dates. "And this is . . . ?" He turned to Auntie Lea.

Her eyes were glowing. "It's our family tree, kiddo. Vesper's helping me get this together. Pretty cool, huh?" Auntie Lea rocked on her stool, hands on hips as she admired the board. She was wearing faded jeans and a paint-stained denim shirt. There was dust in her hair. But she was positively bubbling. He had witnessed a lot of her moods, but bubbly was a new one. Trace liked history and the idea of tracing their ancestors—to an extent. But clearly not as much as Auntie Lea did.

"Eeeeeeek!" Auntie Lea jumped. So did Trace. Vesper did not budge. "I gotta change. Vesper, hold down the fort! Theo, um, you, um . . . You're in charge. Just help Vesper with whatever she needs and I'll be right back." Auntie Lea raced from the kitchen and ran up the stairs to her room.

Trace looked at Vesper.

"Hmmmmm," Vesper said.

"Hmmmmmm?" Trace asked.

This day really could not get weirder. He took the metal box from his pocket and set it on the table so he would remember to give it to his aunt. The aunt who had no clue that his coming home early was unusual. The aunt who had no idea that these projects of hers might seem a bit strange to a normal person. And the aunt who clearly did not have the slightest notion that he was the last person to put in charge of anything.

"We probably should clear off the table," Vesper said, rising from her stool and stretching. "I'll help and then I'm outa here, okay?" She smiled warmly at Trace. Together, they slid loose pictures back into photo albums, loaded the albums into the basket, and balanced it on one of the stools. Vesper was sneaking weird glances his way, twisting her lips occasionally as though she was screwing the lid down on a jar full of words. Weird. But Trace just wanted to go upstairs, drop his books, climb onto his bed, and figure out exactly when and how this day had slipped off the leash. He was in charge. Right. So he would wait for Auntie Lea, give her the box, and *then* escape to his room.

An aria he actually recognized poured out of the speakers. Luciano Pavarotti was singing "Nessun Dorma." Opera had been one notch above polka music in his opinion, but he had grown to like certain pieces since he had come to live in Brooklyn. This was one of them. After about the sixtieth time she played it, Auntie Lea had read him a translation of the lyrics and one line had caught him off guard. *Ma il mio mistero è chiuso in me*: "But my secret lies hidden within me." It was just some Italian guy crooning about not having the guts to tell a woman he loved her, but the melody got to him. And that line stung every time Trace heard it.

"Where d'you keep the place mats, Theo?" Vesper asked. Trace pulled himself out of the music. He found two place mats and laid them out as Vesper pulled glasses from the cabinet.

"You may have noticed that your aunt's a little, uh . . . ," Vesper said over her shoulder.

"Bubbly?" Trace offered.

Vesper chuckled. "Yep, bubbly. Perfect." She rinsed out a couple of wineglasses, grabbed a towel, and slowly dried them as she studied Trace.

"Here's the thing," she continued. "I haven't seen her like this in quite a while." Vesper paused and screwed up her face again as though trying to decide if she should continue. "Okay. Well, this *guy* came over this morning to fix the bed. That awful creak? So, he's a carpenter-slash-handyman kinda guy, you know?"

Trace nodded, unsure where this was headed.

"Well, I was here helping her get started on this family tree and he stays for lunch even though, if you ask *me*, the creak in that bed had been *done* been fixed." Vesper raised her eyebrows meaningfully, but Trace wasn't sure what that meant.

"So, I'm getting ready to go, but your aunt invites this total stranger to stay for dinner . . . and the man skips outa here to go get 'provisions.' That's what he said, 'provisions.' Says he's gonna cook up a 'mean cacciatore' for her." Vesper began rifling through the silverware drawer, pulling out more forks and knives than they would ever need.

"All right . . . ," Trace began. "So, he's coming back

and you're not staying, and what? Are you telling me that you think he's dangerous or something?"

"Ha!" Vesper dropped a handful of utensils on the table. "You got cloth napkins somewhere?"

That was not exactly an answer. Trace pulled napkins from a drawer near the sink and slapped them onto the table. What was she saying?

"All men are dangerous," Vesper huffed. "No offense, kid." So she *was* a lesbian. *At least one thing has been cleared up today*, Trace thought.

"Including and starting with my husband."

Trace took a seat at the table.

"Look, Vesper," he said. Apparently, nothing was really what it seemed to be. He felt like he had fallen through a wormhole today, beginning with Presley talking about seeing that kid with him. Trace suddenly felt exhausted. Okay, Vesper wasn't a lesbian. Angel's mom wasn't dead. And he wasn't really the team leader. Fine. "What exactly are you telling me?"

But before she could answer, the doorbell rang and Auntie Lea shouted down the stairs, "Get that, will you, Theo? I'm coming right down."

Vesper motioned for him to stay right where he was.

"I'll get it," she said. "I'm leaving anyway." Coming

over to him, she kissed Trace smack on the forehead. "I think your auntie has a bit of a crush, that's all I'm sayin'." Vesper put a chubby finger to her lips. "You didn't hear this from me, okay? But she was acting all girly around him. And, darlin', I don't blame her one bit, 'cause the man is *fi-i-i-i-ine*!" Vesper danced toward the door, grabbing her coat from the rack in the hall as she passed it.

Just as Vesper opened the front door, his aunt came sailing down the stairs. A blast of cold air rushed in from the hall, carrying with it the scent of the musk oil that Auntie Lea wore on special occasions. Trace heard a man's voice but, from where he sat, he could only see his aunt's back, covered now in a soft velvet tunic that she wore over what she called her palazzo pants. Auntie Lea had a crush. Trace grinned to himself.

Then in walked Dallas Houston.

One of the weirdest things Trace had ever heard was about *white*. Red plus yellow makes orange. Okay. Mix blue and red and you get purple. Fine. Yellow and blue make green . . . he could see that. But Miss Ledbetter, the art teacher at his old school, insisted not only that white was a color, but that it was what you got when every color was present. That was just nuts. She had called black the absence of all colors, but white, she claimed, was every color combined. Maybe it was a racial thing. Maybe she was speaking symbolically or ironically or metaphorically—one of those English Lit ways where what you say is not necessarily what you mean. But one day Miss Ledbetter had also proudly showed off a sweater she had knitted out of dog's hair that she had plucked off her couch. Miss Ledbetter's sweater smelled like a hamster cage. Miss Ledbetter was not someone Trace believed.

But when Dallas Houston walked into the kitchen at 810 Vanderbilt Avenue, Brooklyn, planet Earth, Trace's brain exploded. And every color really *was* in the white light that filled his head. Up popped the red-faced library guard, Ms. Levy in her dark-blue bike helmet, Ty's yellow backpack as he walked away in the subway station, Dr. Proctor's cool green hushed office, the dark-brown face of the little boy, the splatter of colors on Auntie Lea's jewelry table—and the small orange card. That card he had folded into a projectile. The little airplane he had sent flying and forgotten about. Auntie Lea had found Dallas Houston's card, unfolded it, and actually called the guy. His aunt probably considered it Fate. She would have read it as a sign from the cosmos. But what it *was* was messed up. This was not supposed to happen.

"This is Theo," Auntie Lea was saying as the man's hand came his way. Trace watched his own hand float up to shake it. Definitely not good. "And Theo, this is Dallas Houston. He managed to fix that squeaky leg on my bed, and *now*, he's offered to fix us a gourmet dinner." Auntie Lea was sort of chirping as she talked, and she never stopped smiling at Dallas.

Trace heard himself say something like, "Mrrph-hff." He was so busted.

"What's this?" Auntie Lea asked, picking up the box on the table.

Trace blinked. "Oh, Mr., uh, Roman sent you this. I . . . I saw him on my way home and he wanted me to give it to you," Trace heard himself say. And then he waited. He stopped breathing and just waited. Waited for Dallas Houston to rat him out to Auntie Lea.

# 14

*Cacciatore* in Italian means "hunter." According to Dallas Houston, hunters would make this dish with any kind of meat they could catch or trap or sneak up on or just burst through the front door and ambush. Trace was feeling a lot of sympathy for the chicken that was being hacked into chunks on a cutting board.

Dallas had insisted that Auntie Lea "go relax" while the men did the cooking. And his aunt, thrilled to find that Roman's box held a handful of antique metal beads, had danced happily off to her worktable, lugging Aunt Frenchy's basket of junk. Unbelievable. On the one hand, Trace was glad she had left before Dallas could start babbling about ghosts. On the other hand, the man was a complete weirdo, a total stranger she had handed a meat cleaver to and left with her only nephew.

"Small planet, huh?" Dallas said now, over his shoulder.

Trace said nothing. Maybe he could cut a deal. This guy had no idea what talk about ghosts would do to Auntie Lea. He really, really, *reallllllly* did not want to think about, describe, or endlessly revisit every minute detail that she would quiz him about.

"I'm guessing you didn't give your aunt my card?" the man tried again. He handed Trace a bag of mushrooms, a knife, and another cutting board. Before he could answer, Dallas added, "Because she said something about the cosmos just dropping it in her lap."

"I, uh . . . ," Trace began. As angrily as he had folded that card into a plane, he had not cared less about where it might have landed. Until now. "I must've left your card out somewhere. And, well, my room is her, uh, Auntie Lea makes jewelry and . . ."

Dallas turned, leaned against the sink, and crossed his arms over his chest. On the stove, the chicken sizzled noisily in onions and peppers and olive oil. Trace wanted to escape to his room and avoid dinner altogether. But he was getting pretty hungry. They needed to have this out now. Why did Dallas Houston shake his hand and act like they had never met? Why had he not told Auntie Lea how that business card just *happened* to appear? Taking a deep breath, Trace gave the man the hardest don't-mess-with-me look he could muster. "Okay," he said. "What do you want?"

The salad that Trace had pulled together looked a lot more cheerful than he felt. Dallas had agreed to keep quiet about ghosts. And Trace had agreed to go back to the library on Saturday, back to the stacks to help Dallas look for the kid.

"I believe there's a reason you got a good look at him like you did. All these years I've been down there, most I get is a feeling, a flicker at the edge of my eyesight. Once, I thought I saw him kinda wandering between the stacks, like he was lookin' for something." Dallas paused, shook his head, and turned toward the stove. "Always make me sad when that little guy shows up," he added. Pouring a boiling pot of bow-tie pasta into a colander, the man's face reddened as a cloud of steam enveloped it.

The air in the kitchen was warm and damp now.

Trace felt his mind pulling him down, down into the shadowy underground stacks, down where ghosts walked, down, he was afraid, into the river. If anyone dead wanted to contact him, he thought he knew who it would be.

"Hey, Signore!" Auntie Lea sang, gliding into the kitchen and interrupting his descent. "Grab a glass." She uncorked a bottle of wine just as Dallas pulled a loaf of crusty bread from the oven. "Ooooooh," she sighed. "I can resist anything except the smell of butter . . . or garlic . . . or bread." She giggled like a little girl. "Or buttered garlic bread." Placing a pair of candlesticks on the table, she lit two new candles and then, all smiles, filled two glasses. With a wink at Trace, she poured him a little as well.

The thought of ghost hunting should have ruined his appetite, but Trace was starving. And the smell of the wine only seemed to make him hungrier. Unlike when the Cuties came to dinner and made a point of quizzing or teasing him, it was easy to keep a low profile with Dallas around. Trace dug into the pasta and chicken and let the adults chatter, happy to steer his mind away from the shadows. The wine did not taste as good as he had thought it would, but when Auntie

Lea poured another round, she gave him a bit more. Watching her and Dallas, it occurred to him that the game never got easier. They were dancing around each other with words, inching closer, comparing likes and dislikes, testing their fit. Maybe it was the wine that made this so clear. Trace turned the bottle around and blinked at the label. This glass tasted better than the first, but it looked like it was the same stuff.

Dallas began talking about where to find the freshest ingredients. Auntie Lea talked about the vegetable garden she intended to plant in the backyard. That was news. Dallas worried that the cacciatore needed more pepper. Auntie Lea, who Trace had never seen eat meat, oohed and aahed her way through two bowlfuls. By the time they had moved on to wines and Italy and which regions produced the best olive oil, mozzarella, leather, and stained glass, Trace had polished off his salad. The conversation veered off into sculpture and tapestries while the candles flickered between Dallas and his aunt. Trace watched them smile easily at each other, lean in, and grow misty-eyed as they nodded in sad agreement that wood carving was, tragically, a lost art. That made them both sigh so loudly that Trace had to bite the rim of his glass to stifle a laugh.

Auntie Lea refilled the wineglasses, pouring Trace just a "teensy" bit more. She murmured something about kids in Europe drinking wine at dinner every single night. "And do *they* become mass murderers or drug addicts? I don't think so!" she asked and answered merrily. It occurred to Trace that he had never seen her drink wine either.

Auntie Lea and Dallas zinged from topic to topic. There was music they both liked, movies they hated. Countries they had visited and strange foods they had encountered. Dallas mentioned monkey brains. Auntie Lea had eaten chocolate-covered ants. Trace finished the little that was left of his wine, broke off and bit into another slice of bread. The garlicky smell of the cold, congealed butter only hit him as he swallowed and a doughy lump of bread stuck in his throat. Trace suddenly felt close to tears. Everything turned cold, didn't it? No matter how nice something was, just give it time. Somewhere, in the back of his head, he knew it was ridiculous to let this make him feel so sad. He was stuffed. His head felt floaty. Would it be rude to just rest it on the table for a minute? he wondered.

The candles had burned low. Dallas and Auntie Lea moved seamlessly from the art of stone carving to funny gravestone inscriptions . . . *Here lies Lester Moore. Four slugs from a forty-four. No Les. No More . . .* The two of them dissolved into laughter at that, but the sound of it seemed to reach Trace through wads of cotton. Enough. No way was he listening to grave talk. Not funny. Trace pushed himself up from the table and clumsily maneuvered his dishes into the sink. Silverware slipped from his hands, splattering sauce and clattering loudly onto his bowl. Mumbling a "good night" that he was pretty sure went unheard, Trace tilted his way dizzily up the stairs and, with a bit of difficulty, into his bed.

His eyebrows hurt. Just peeling one eye open took some work. Trace's head seemed to be stuck to the pillow, and only with some effort and in slow motion could he roll over to check his alarm clock. He realized his vision was fuzzy, but it still really looked like it was past eleven a.m. Sitting up quickly brought on a whole new wave of eyebrow-related pain. Trace gave the clock another chance. It was 11:22 a.m. From far, far away he could hear someone groaning. He was about three hours past seriously screwed.

Massaging his temples, Trace remembered the

wine. Auntie Lea was clueless. And, yes, he had known better, even if she didn't *yet*. He should've schooled her about what his mom would have thought about him drinking wine. And he would. But first, he had to unstick his head from his pillow. If possible. He would never make it as an alcoholic.

Someone, somewhere, groaned again as Trace crawled through his covers, slid himself around, then tipped his legs carefully off the mattress, toes gingerly searching out each rung as he clutched the ladder tightly. He had no memory of turning off his alarm clock. Or setting it. Or climbing up to the loft bed. And absolutely no idea how the mess piled on the floor around Auntie Lea's worktable got there. As he stepped cautiously around frayed photo albums, over crumpled handkerchiefs and scattered jewelry, Trace winced, suddenly recalling the loud crash when his hip had collided with Aunt Frenchy's basket last night.

No time to waste though; he would clean it up later. Trace dressed hurriedly, scrolling through plausible excuses as he yanked on his jeans. What if he had an early-morning dentist appointment, or how about if he had been mugged on his way to school? That could happen. His socks from yesterday, draped on the back of a chair, passed the smell test and he sat down to tug them on. Maybe he could say that he had rescued a kitten from a tree or, even better, a baby from a burning building. No. Not good. A flaming baby would show up on TV. He needed something no one could check.

He swung his backpack over his shoulder and ran downstairs. There was no sign of Auntie Lea. Grabbing an apple and a box of juice for the subway, Trace hurried out so quickly that he nearly collided with an old lady who was inching her grocery cart past his building. She let out a little squeak when he stopped short, but Trace could have kissed her. This was perfect! A little old lady had gotten knocked down in the street and he had come to her rescue and helped her home. Best of all, little old ladies are known to be extremely slow-moving, so it had taken him all morning. He would be a real, live Good Samaritan. He might have to dodge a few questions, but wasn't it better than saying he was out cold with a hangover? Duh.

By the time he reached Myrtle Avenue, Trace had thrown in a few convincing details, but not *too* many. Offering too much random information, his mom said, was a dead giveaway. He had never felt comfortable about lying. But polishing his little old lady story was beginning to make him feel kind of heroic.

"Trace!" He froze. That *sounded* like his name, but it was a girl's voice. He quickly dismissed the thought of truant officers: They were just an urban myth, right?

"Hey, Trace!"

Turning toward the voice, he felt a smile spread across his face and seep right through his whole body. Angel, the goddess, was across the street, leaning out of the door at Roman's Hardware and waving him over. And then Trace was floating across Myrtle Avenue. Angel was waiting for him. For *him*. A swish of air passed behind him and a taxi driver yelled something at him in Spanish. A bus honked as he hopped onto the curb. But all that Trace noticed was that, from close up, she was even prettier than he remembered. And when she smiled, she was beautiful.

"Hey, Angel." Trace grinned. Wasn't he supposed to *be* somewhere?

# 15

Who *was* he? Cutting class, drinking wine, making up lies, and now this. But he felt good. *Reallllllly* good. Leaning back on the bouncy metal garden chair, Trace gently bobbed to the music flooding through his head. Angel called it *salsa*. Above him, tree branches waved, their red and gold leaves parting to show off crisp blue patches. Neon-white clouds were moving across the sky at an unhurried pace. He saw a giraffe, poking its head out of the sunroof of a Volkswagen Beetle. Then he watched as the cloud slowly morphed into a turtle with a saxophone. *Okay, next cloud*, Trace thought, grinning as the cloud complied and moved along.

"Hey, mister," Angel said. She pulled her earphones

off Trace's head and handed him a soda. Before him, on a low table studded with tiles, she had placed a tray of chips and dips, cheese and cookies. Trace suddenly realized he was starving. Even if it had occurred to him that Roman's Hardware had a backyard, he would not have imagined this paradise. Beyond the brooms and shovels, past a wall hung with hammers and pliers and wrenches, Angel had led him to a door that appeared to be just another closet. It was like the entrance to Narnia. Hanging just below the ceiling, where it could be seen through the doorway by anyone in the garden, was a screen showing the front of the store and the cash register. Angel was on duty, but no customers had come in since Trace had arrived.

"'Kay," Angel continued. "Lemme find this other song that you have *got* to hear." She clamped the earphones on her head and began scrolling through her playlists. Angel's school was having Teacher Development Day, so her dad had her minding the store. Trace brightened. Maybe his school was out too? Maybe he wasn't cutting? Then he remembered getting out early the day before. That had been for a teachers' thing. They only got half a day, though. No fair.

Trace scooped up handfuls of chips, washed them

down with a swig of soda, and started on the cookies. Against a side wall, a small, rocky waterfall was embedded in a row of bushes. Weeds and wilting flowers were poking up around an army of bluish-green frog statues that seemed to be guarding it. Between the burbling fountain, an occasional birdcall, and whatever tune Angel was humming, Trace felt as if he were deep in a forest. "This is the one," Angel said, tugging the earphones off. "I have to stock some stuff that just came in before my dad gets back. You okay out here by yourself?"

Trace surveyed the feast before him.

"Breakfast is *the* most important meal of the day," he said, pretty sure that was a witty response.

"Dude, you are *so* weird." Angel laughed. Ruffling his hair a bit, she clamped the headphones on his head, then pulled one side away from his ear. "If this doesn't make you want to dance, nothing will." With a wink, Angel hit Play and left him with the music. Trace was not about to dance. Here? In front of her? Well, in her backyard when any moment she might look out and see him? Nope. In his room, he could dance. His moves were legendary. Crowd-shocking. Poetic, even. But he needed his own beats. This music *was* good, though.

He couldn't understand a word the singers were chanting. Trace realized he was beating out the rhythm on his knees. All right, Mr. Theodore Raymond Carter: here you are, hanging with an older woman, cutting school, and very possibly hungover. He leaned back against the chair, needing to anchor his head to something solid. It did feel heavy, but dangerously buoyant and soft too, like a hot air balloon that might take off for parts unknown if its ropes didn't hold.

"They would totally kill me. Drinking wine? Cutting class?" Trace said softly, shaking his head. "Yep, kill me dead." Trace squinted at the monitor hanging in the doorway that gave an occasional glimpse of Angel, stepping behind the counter to make notes on a pad. With the whole day off, her dad had left her in charge while he ran errands. Roman trusted her with his whole store.

"They'd kill me." He sighed. But then, *they* wouldn't kill him. Because *they* were gone. If anything, he had killed them. Trace pressed his eyes closed.

Just the thought made his throat grow tight. He tried to swallow. But the river . . . that lump of murky, olive-brown river bottom . . . was stuck there again, trying to go down, pressing against his throat. Trace felt his heart start racing like crazy. Telling himself *not* to panic was making him break out in a sweat. Trace focused on the music, willed himself to sink into the bass line that was thumping like a heartbeat. The rhythm, hypnotic and warm, made him wish he'd studied Spanish. He wanted to sing and dance and, maybe, to whisk Angel along with him. Nice. Trace leaned back, checked the clouds, and let the music wrap snugly around him. The river couldn't touch him.

In fact, he was surprised to realize that he *wanted* to think about the river. It was just a crummy little river. Why should he avoid it? The song ended and another one began, slower, with a rolling melody. A perfect soundtrack, Trace thought, floating along with the music, safely above everything. He could tune in or tune out, it could all be just a reality show . . . starring himself. With a smile, he leaned back, eyes closed, the better to see everything.

So there they all were, laughing on the drive to North Carolina even though they were heading to a funeral. Mom and Dad were singing along to tunes on the radio, making up any lyrics they didn't remember and telling stories that went with every song: whose party they had been at, what J.Lo or Jay-Z or Will Smith had done lately; Trace had escaped to his iPod, only removing his headphones when they stopped for gas and snacks. Now he felt a slight twinge: he would never know those stories.

Dad's timing had been perfect, pulling up to the church just before the service. A picture of Aunt Frenchy, with a long silver braid coiled atop her head, sat on an easel at the entrance. Trace had only met her when he was a baby. In the data bank that was his brain, Françoise Raymond Minor, the older of his mom's two aunts, was an empty file. As Auntie Lea would say, he wouldn't know her if she sat on his lap on the F train. The thought of a frail little woman plopping onto his lap in the subway made him wince.

Despite what he had expected, the funeral had been anything but sad. His grandmother, Maman DeLeon, had smothered him in a hug and immediately put him to work handing out brochures as people arrived and running to the church basement to grab extra hymnals or to find someone to crank up the air-conditioning. There had been music and funny stories and a lot of talk about Aunt Frenchy "going home." Only now and then were there tears. It was Trace's first funeral. "But not my last," he said into a passing breeze.

A wave of warm water seemed to wash over him and Trace felt as if his whole body was crying. But that's okay, the music said. "*Latigo, latigo, latigo*," a singer crooned. *Let it go, let it go, let it go*, Trace repeated. Wait. Had he been singing out loud? Opening his eyes, he was glad to see that Angel was behind the counter ringing up a purchase. A smiling customer shifted the baby bundled against her chest so that she could pull out her purse. Trace saw a tiny hand reach up to rest against the woman's sleeve, making a pale splotch on the monitor. He closed his eyes, ready to get back to his own reality show, seeing himself wrapped in Maman DeLeon's arms . . . how softly he had been folded into them, how powdery she was.

After the funeral, there had been a repast—which he learned just meant food and more food . . . brought by people who crammed into Maman's small house to tell Aunt Frenchy tales. Trace saw himself in the line moving slowly past bowls of potato salad and mac and cheese, platters of deviled eggs, apple pies and peach cobblers. "Comfort food," Auntie Lea had called it, making Trace add collard greens to a plate already piled high with grilled chicken and biscuits.

Whenever his mom and her sister got together, they would pull out photo albums, and in Maman DeLeon's bedroom closet they had struck gold. By the afternoon, with Trace wedged between them, nearly submerged in the pillow-soft couch, they had leafed through every last album, holding him captive. He remembered staring at the creased photo of a spindly little girl, his grandmother, with the caption *Seraphina DeLeon, age five*. She was so tiny.

"*That's Maman?*" he had asked in amazement. His mom and Auntie Lea had laughed at his disbelief. Now Maman was *soooo* big and *soooo* soft and *soooo* wrinkly. "Everyone gets old," his mom had said.

Trace leaned back, looked at the sky for a minute, then closed his eyes again. "Wrong there, Mom," he said quietly. "Not everyone."

Trace could see them packing up the car, saying their good-byes, and hitting the road. His dad had hoped to make it to Baltimore before rush hour, but as they merged onto the highway Trace realized that he was missing his iPod. "*Don't say it,*" Trace tried to warn himself, but he knew how this played out. He heard himself say that they *had* to go back. *Yes*, he had checked his bag and his pockets. *No*, he could not wait for Maman to mail it: he needed his iPod for the trip home.

His dad had taken the first exit, crossed the overpass, and swung the car into a southbound lane. "It'll just take a minute," Trace promised.

"It's all good," his dad had said. That was his mom and dad's favorite saying. Their way of letting him know everything was cool, even this delay. His mom winked at him over her shoulder and cranked up the air conditioner. They were in no real hurry.

But this, *this* was the moment in time that Trace knew he would do over. This was the answer to Dr. Proctor's time travel question. He would have left it behind. It was just a stupid iPod. But he had made them go back.

And if they had not? Tick. Tick. Tick. What if they had stayed five minutes more? Tick. Five minutes less? Tick. There was Maman on the porch again and Auntie Lea laughing, knowing one of them must have forgotten something. Maman rattling off his dad's favorite dishes, trying to persuade them to stay for dinner, to sleep over. Tick. More hugs all around. Tick.

Tick. Questionable promises to call, to write, to email, to visit more often. Tick. Tick. Tick. More of the stuff people do who expect to see each other again. This was nice. He could see them all together again one more time. It felt like he had the power to eavesdrop on that day.

"Drive safely. Call me when you're home," Maman had called out. Trace nodded. "When we're home," he repeated to the tree branches overhead, to the clouds. And then they were at the bridge. From the back seat, the river had looked small, like nothing special. But the car had jerked suddenly, swerving to miss the brown flash of a deer bounding out of the trees before the bridge. And then they were in a world of slow motion. And absolute silence. Never again would anything be so crystal clear.

There was the guardrail. Gray and chipped, dented metal. They were going to hit it. It would stop them. Oh. The flimsy guardrail had crumpled. Wow. Now they were sailing. Gracefully, slowly, his book bag took flight. He watched the deliberate arc it traveled only to slam against the window. Mom's sunglasses pirouetted silently over her shoulder. Dad's paperback sailed toward him, launching its bookmark into the air. HEY! That first bump had shaken his rib cage, sucked all the air out of his lungs. Tumbling now, and rolling into—WHOMP! Trace was yanked hard against his seat belt. The second bump really hurt. "That's going to bruise." Trace grimaced, glad to be just watching, not to actually be there for this part.

Whoa! The water, already? This would be the rough part, and Trace tried to breathe with the music, hold on to the rhythm. Because he already knew that those windows were crap. And here came the water, rising right up through the floor, out from the dashboard, curling in around the window seams. No amount of jabbing the Down button on the handle mattered. Dad kicking the glass like crazy didn't work. Should he have kicked too?

The water was up to his chin. She'd be there soon. It reached his nose. Then there she was, her hands wrapping around his arms, grasping him, not that gently, and steering him right through the window. The sick olive-brown water kept churning around them; it was gritty with dirt from the riverbed as it streamed away from the sinking car. There was that familiar thumping in his chest as the river tried to hold on to him. But those strong brown arms that had pulled him were pushing him toward the surface now. *I've got you*. She had not spoken but he had heard her. *I've come back for you*.

Angel touched his knee and Trace bolted upright out of the chair. "Whoa, dude," she said, laughing nervously. "You okay?" Hot tears stung the corners of his eyes, so Trace massaged them away roughly, hoping it would look like he was coming out of a deep sleep. NO way would Angel see him cry. Turning his head, he stretched and yawned dramatically to cover himself as he wiped his cheeks on his sleeves. "I'm good. I'm cool," he croaked.

"Papi's on his way back," Angel said. She scooped up the cookie plate and the bowl of salsa. "Don't leave any mess out here, okay?" she said, dusting a few chips off his knee. "I'll get busted for snacking on the job."

Trace jumped up quickly at her touch, yanking off the headphones and scattering more chips in the process. "Hey," he said, trying to sound cool, "just don't you bust *me* for cutting school, okay?"

"Deal." Angel laughed. And then she was right in front of him, smelling like the garden and leaning in for a kiss. Or at least he *thought* she wanted to kiss him. Maybe she had aimed for his cheek. Maybe she just wanted to whisper something. But, surprised by her sudden closeness, Trace turned and caught the side of her lips with his. And then he knew.

The girl was seriously beautiful. And she did like him, and not just as a friend. He should kiss her now, full on, just to let her know that he was cool with this. Because somewhere deep in his chest, a switch had been flipped and Trace was lighting up, ears to toes. So what if she was older, or lived in the Bronx? How far could that be on the subway? He would kiss her now, a real kiss so she would know it was okay. And he did.

"Whoa, *awkward*," Angel giggled, lurching backward. "Just wanted to grab the cans. No offense, dude." Angel had an amused frown on her face. "We good?"

Trace coughed. "Man, that music was, um, thanks for the, uh . . ." He realized he was muttering gibberish. "I'm just, uh, sorry about that, it just . . ."

Angel poked him gently in the ribs with her elbow. "Grab the bag of chips, will ya, Romeo?" she said, laughing, and headed into the store.

The apartment was quiet when he got home. Trace went straight to his room, dropped his book bag on his desk, and fished out the envelope he kept tucked in the bottom drawer. Now was a good time. Maybe Angel had not meant to kiss him, but he could swear that for a second there, she had kissed him back. So, as long as he didn't think about the world of trouble waiting at school for him tomorrow, this had been a good day.

He opened the envelope, paused only a second to take a breath, then pulled out the article and pressed it open on his desk. Under the headline *Boy, 13, Only Survivor of Tragic Plunge from Saville Bridge* was a photo of their badly dented car being dragged from the water. Trace instantly remembered the feel of the wet riverbank, the muddy water draining out of his sneakers, as he sat on the edge of a gurney, unwilling to lie down like the EMT worker had asked him to do. He had just kept watching the water.

Only after he was in the hospital, hooked up to monitors that blinked or beeped nonstop messages to the nurses and doctors who buzzed around him, did the questions begin. Did he know what day it was? Monday. Could he tell them his name? Theodore Carter. Did he know where he was? Yes. Had his parents been drinking? No. What made them swerve off the road? A deer. How had he gotten out of the car? How had he gotten out of the car? How *had* he gotten out of the car?

The sun was setting and his room filled with a soft orange light. Trace looked at the photo again, relieved that the dark shapes inside the car revealed nothing. There was no glint from a shirt button or edge of a collar, thank God, no distinct profile that might crush him if he recognized it. But the article had been clear about one thing, and sure enough, the photo was too: every window in the car was completely closed.

# 16

Vanderbilt Avenue was crawling with zombies. A little frog hopped by, trying to keep up with a woman who was staring at her phone, oblivious to the two-legged slice of pizza and miniature cowgirl coming up behind her. Trace rounded the corner onto Myrtle Avenue, merging with throngs of kids in costumes and parents in somber work clothes, all heading for school or buses or subway trains.

He was a big believer in free candy, but Brooklyn's celebration of the holiday seemed like Halloween, the viral version. With one day left to go, it looked like every school in Brooklyn had planned a party for Friday. He had *meant* to get up early and run through his presentation, double-check some dates and names and time everything. Trace spotted the huge clock on the bank at the corner of Clinton Avenue, its every minute marked with a shiny brass bar. Of course! There was no time. Why had he even been sweating this? The class was only an hour long. So, at fifteen minutes per team, maybe they would make it to the 1860s today . . . and maybe pigs could fly, he thought with relief.

Hurrying across the intersection, he looked up and saw that a lumpy pink pig with feathery wings was stumbling toward him, muttering loudly and wrestling with a freckled-face vampire over control of a plastic pumpkin. The flying pig was winning. Trace shook his head. Okay, pigs *might* fly today. Auntie Lea could be right: the universe *does* send us messages. But an hour was still only sixty minutes. Even in Mrs. Weaver's class.

Trace felt great. On Wednesday, he had come home to a note from Auntie Lea taped on the refrigerator door.

*Dear Theo,*

*Sorry to miss you. Let you sleep in today (but we gotta have the WINE talk later). I'm out till*

*waaaaay late tonight . . . don't you dare wait up!*
*$$$ on the counter for a pizza or whatever, okay?*
*Doing a HUMONGOUS shoot for the Vaca-*
*tioners . . . Wait till you hear their new tracks . . .*
*v. cool music.*

*Love, yer flaky aunt.*

After all the versions of the story that he had rehearsed on the way home from Roman's, no explanation had been necessary. And Thursday morning, although he had awoken early to try to pull his report together, Auntie Lea must have gotten up even earlier and left. Because two notes had been stuck to his bedroom door. One was addressed to "To whom it may concern," and it wasn't sealed. Trace guessed that Auntie Lea wanted him to read it so that their stories would match. She had written that he had not "been well enough" to attend school on Wednesday. That left him a lot of wiggle room should anyone ask for details. Her second note had said, "Tried to wake you, but not *tooo* hard. We'll talk later, kiddo."

Thursday had been gray and rainy and cold. In the school office, no one had even looked up when he delivered Auntie Lea's note. Clearly, he had not been missed. He had seen Presley from a distance, flying out of the cafeteria just as he had arrived. And Kali had ignored him in the hallway, twice, which was normal. By afternoon, he knew that not running into Ty all day had been no accident. They had no classes together on Thursdays but they usually met up after school. So Trace had lingered at the deli, watching until the last of the stragglers from school had filed into the subway.

At least it was finally Friday. After his team gave their report, if Ty didn't want to talk to him, fine.

The bus stop was still a block and a half away when he caught sight of the #54 bus lurching along Myrtle behind him. Breaking into a trot, Trace dodged fairies, robots, and pirates, keeping one hand firmly clamped on his jacket pocket. The little metal rattle from Aunt Frenchy's basket was tucked away safely there, his secret weapon. Now that he thought about it, the rusty toy was probably the first sign from the universe that things would go his way today. Roman had thought that the toy came from the 1840s, which made it a genuine pre–Civil War artifact. Everyone else could trot out copies of old photographs, but this was the real deal. Even if they got an extra weekend to prepare, Kali would have a hard time finding something this good if she wanted to one-up him this time.

Trace reached the bus stop at the same time as the bus and lined up behind a massive woman in a hot-pink sweat suit. Climbing onto the bus in front of her was the sixteenth president, Abraham Lincoln, decked out in a black topcoat, stovepipe hat, book bag, and . . . fluorescent orange sneakers? Trace watched as Abe swiped a MetroCard and headed for the rear of the bus, giving him a quick look at the face under the hat. Presley? The fuzzy black beard dangling loosely from her ears swung toward the back of the bus before she did. It was definitely Presley.

Trace rarely left early enough to enjoy the luxury of taking the bus to school. He had hoped that the nice long bus ride would give him time to think through his presentation. Maybe he should duck Presley. He watched as she slid into an empty row of seats near the rear and, with some effort, disconnected herself from her book bag. Trace was about to squeeze into what remained of the seat next to Pink Sweat Suit when he saw Presley look up, flash a big smile, and point frantically at the empty seat next to her. So much for peace and quiet. Trace worked his way down the aisle. Up close, Presley appeared to have three eyebrows. One of her bushy Abraham Lincoln paste-on eyebrows was perched like a disheveled black caterpillar just below the brim of her hat.

"Impressive," Trace said, sliding into the seat. "Let me guess—you're a Goth pizza chef?"

"Don't be farcical." Presley laughed, clearly delighted to have company. Hugging the book bag on her lap, she stared up at him and wriggled her nose dramatically. "This beard itches like crazy," she confessed. "But I want to be dexterous, zealous, and proficient, even if we don't have to give our report today."

This was exactly why Trace had hoped to dodge her.

"Ready, willing, and able, silly." Presley giggled, shoving a bony elbow into his side. The Lincoln caterpillars bobbled merrily.

"Um, look," she said quietly. "Sorry about giving you a hard time the other day. I know you were just trying to help me."

Trace was not sure what to say. So he said nothing.

"I just get so tired of everyone treating me like a kid, you know? Kali's a pain sometimes, but I can take care of myself." Presley was frowning so hard that the caterpillars nearly touched. "I'm only a year younger than you guys, but I'm very, *very* mature for my age, all right?"

"Okay, Presley," Trace said, trying not to grin. A smell of shoe polish hovered around her head, and the black electrical tape that was holding down the lid on her stovepipe hat was peeling off in the back, revealing a patch of red. The very mature Presley was wearing a carton of Quaker oatmeal on her head.

For Trace, the fifteen-minute ride to Jay Street took hours with Presley babbling nonstop. He learned that Ty was planning to dress as Alexander Graham Bell, that Kali would absolutely, positively, *categorically* not be in costume, and that he would be the last one in their group to give a presentation. Without him there, it seemed that their rehearsal on Wednesday had gone very smoothly. When the bus finally jerked to a stop at their corner, Trace threaded his way through a wall of passengers and climbed off, Presley scrambling down the steps right behind him.

"So, I was a little, um, perturbed when you didn't come to school on Wednesday, and then I didn't see you yesterday either," she said. Presley pulled on her backpack as she walked, the bulky sleeves of her black overcoat making it hard for her to navigate the straps.

Looking straight ahead, Trace kept a steady pace, a pace meant to signal that he would not slow down for her—but he wasn't abandoning her either. He just wanted time alone to think. It would be fine if he went last, in fact; that was cool. Kali had all the good stuff about Jesse James and the Pony Express anyway. But when it was his turn, should he do the Jim Crow and KKK stuff first and *then* the draft riots? They really had stuck him with all the depressing history.

"I thought maybe you were sick? Or had an accident or something horrific had happened?" Presley's voice usually went up at the end of each sentence, so Trace was never sure if she was asking him something or just making a statement.

"'Cause I get these, um, feelings—these *palpitations*—they're like electricity almost, since when I was little," she went on. "I know people may think I'm kinda anomalistic or deviant or just plain weird? So I mostly, well, I keep things to myself, you know?" Presley was puffing now, trying to keep up.

Trace did not know. Trace did not *want* to know. These last few blocks seemed to stretch for miles. He decided that he should definitely lead with the KKK and stick Jim Crow in the middle. That way, he could end with the draft riots, pulling out the toy as a real, live artifact. Did he *have* to talk about the orphanage? Just the word made him think of the chilly darkness spreading underneath the library. All those little kids. All those shadows. Row after row of things just out of sight: clouded shapes that shifted when you looked at them, faint sounds that you *almost* heard. And that awful smell of cold, wet earth. It had smelled like . . . like the river bottom down there. And, just like that, the little boy's face, bathed in red light, floated into his mind. Trace felt queasy.

"It kinda freaks out the progenitors, you know?" Presley was chattering away breathlessly at his side. Trace could feel her watching him. But rather than answer her, he began walking faster.

"I've always been able to pick up on stuff. Like that guy who talks to dead people? Kinda like that. And, okay, don't flip out, but there's something or someone around you who—"

"Enough, Presley," Trace said, coming to a full halt and turning to face her. They were on the corner of Atlantic Avenue now, in the thick of the morning rush hour. Aside from the fact that he was standing next to what looked like a runaway munchkin from an insane asylum, nothing could have been more normal or more solid than his surroundings. Stores, traffic, garbage trucks, people everywhere. All the same, he could smell the river and feel the water steadily rising. Only now he had the creepy feeling that Presley was reading his mind, that she had caught him thinking about that little boy. She was frowning at him, her many eyebrows at different angles, watching him as though he were a tightrope walker about to fall at any moment.

"Sorry," she said softly. "Nobody ever wants to know, but I was just worried and . . ." She trailed off.

Trace let her dangle. They walked in silence the last two blocks, Trace lost in uneasy thoughts, Abe Lincoln hot on his heels.

At first, Mrs. Weaver had looked merely confused. But now the teacher was rubbing the sides of her forehead and occasionally letting out a little sigh. Lou Pagano's group had been presenting on the 1850s for twenty-three minutes.

Trace could not stop checking the clock. There was still enough time for his team to be called. Marcus and his 1800s team, in a rapid-fire mumble, had zipped along from the Louisiana Purchase to the creation of the Illinois Territory in under six minutes, making only brief pit stops at the Lewis and Clark expedition, Webster's first dictionary, and Robert Fulton's steamship. And the 1810s had to be skipped entirely because two team members were out with the flu.

The 1820s had brought a wordy, rambling note from Winston's mom blaming computer issues for a delay of his team's "excellent" PowerPoint presentation. Then Haeyoun had asked, in a sugary sweet voice, if the 1830s could postpone their presentation until Monday because they were chasing down some *very* special information.

"All right," Mrs. Weaver had said, to Trace's dismay, "but that's it. No more exceptions, since we will have to wait for the 1840s as well." The teacher gave the class a stern look. The 1840s, all three of them, were in Principal Rivera's office. Mrs. Weaver did not elaborate.

Trace checked the clock again. Two rows away, Presley was doodling blissfully, her stovepipe hat tucked under her chair. On the bus, she had not been at all concerned about having to give their presentation. She must have assumed like he had that there would be no time for their report. But although they were up next, she looked calm and ready to go. He sneaked a look at Kali, across the room. There was a smug smile on her face. She was ready. Trace couldn't see Ty sitting behind him, but he had noticed the pile of color-coded cards on his desk. Ty was ready. Trace ran through his three-minute talk in his head, trying to focus his racing thoughts. He was *so* not ready. Maybe Lou the Schnozz would ramble on right till the end of class, but Mrs. Weaver looked ready to shut him down.

The 1850s had started off okay. Lou had announced that his team members would each report on just one topic: People, Places, or Things of the 1850s. Richie began with Places, stating that San Francisco and LA had officially become cities at the beginning of the decade. Then he had veered off into his top picks for holiday blockbusters due out from Hollywood. His report on Commodore Perry and the US Navy in Japan concluded with the top five reasons why he would *never* eat sushi. When he reached number three: "it's raw," Mrs. Weaver asked the fifties to move on.

Calvin covered Things at a fast clip. The Republican Party was founded, "but it's not a *party* party, you guys," he added. With his next item, the railroad's expansion into the Southwest, Calvin began to sing loudly, "I've Been Working on the Railroad." But Mrs. Weaver shook her head so vigorously, he stopped. "Okay, last thing," he promised. "In the 1850s, both *Moby Dick* and *Uncle Tom's Cabin* were published." Pausing to survey the room, he could barely contain a grin. "One was about a great white and one was about a great black. Get it?" Calvin cracked up. The class was silent. Mrs. Weaver winced.

"Thank you, Calvin," was all she said.

"So I got People, a'ight?" Lou began. "This guy Elisha Otis invents the elevator. Like, *Otis*, get it? Otis elevators. That's why, you guys.

"Then there's Booker T. Washington, who was, like, a slave and whatnot. But check it out: he becomes a big-time leader and writes this totally nonfiction biography called *Up from Slavery* . . . which kinda says it all, right? Cause the guy got *up* . . . from slavery, a'ight?"

Mrs. Weaver massaged her neck. "Thank you for those insights. The 1850s may sit down."

"But I got more, Mrs. W.," Lou insisted. "There's, like, the guy who invented Shredded Wheat and—"

"That'll do, Mr. Pagano," Mrs. Weaver said, coming to her feet so suddenly that Lou jumped. "Your team went over the time limit and we must be fair."

Trace glanced at the clock again and silently thanked Lou.

With only seven minutes left on the clock, Trace relaxed. As Mrs. Weaver reminded the class that the reports would continue on Monday, he pulled out his phone, sliding it under his desk to check his messages. He kept it on mute in class, but he could see the beginning of a text message from Auntie Lea before he even punched in his unlock code: *Read this toot sweet: BEFORE you leave school.*

Auntie Lea never texted him. Trace closed his eyes. What now?

# 17

Trace made a point of arriving at the media center before the others. He'd be there. He'd listen. He'd try to talk to Ty. He knew that this impromptu after-school meeting had been called just to give him an update on how their presentation would go on Monday. If things had been normal, Trace would have let Ty know that Presley had already filled him in. If things had been normal, he and Ty would be headed for the subway now, cracking jokes about Lou's presentation and dodging all the little sugar-crazed gnomes and skeletons heading home from their school parties. If things had been normal, he would have been excited about Auntie Lea's message.

"Hey, Trace, how'd your report go?" Ms. Levy asked. Not surprisingly for a Friday afternoon, the media center was empty. The librarian stopped shelving her overloaded cart of books and was smiling at Trace as though she was happy to have company.

"Oh, hey, Ms. Levy. We only made it as far as the fifties today," he said, grinning. "I'm safe till Monday."

"Hah," she snorted. "'Safe' is overrated, my man." Ms. Levy turned back to the shelves and continued filing books. "Did you ever find out anything about that child who was killed in the draft riot fire?" she asked, throwing the question over her shoulder like a curveball. Like a missile. Trace swallowed. This had to stop. How was it that just a simple question could make his skin go all cold and damp? Why was that lump forming in his throat? His knees felt all rickety suddenly. When would he stop seeing that little boy's wet red eyes? He let out a raspy cough, trying to shake off the clammy, suffocating, thick air he felt gathering around him as he reached for the back of the nearest chair. There was a sudden clattering at the library door, followed by a few exasperated grunts. "H . . . h . . . hello, Ms. Levy," Ty called out as the door opened a crack, closed on him, and then opened again.

A bright-red skateboard had hit the floor and was rolling slowly toward Trace.

Ty juggled his book bag, gym bag, and a juice box with one arm and cradled an overstuffed notebook in the other as he maneuvered the door with his elbow. "Uh, no, Ms. Levy," Trace managed to answer the librarian. "No new news." He went to hold the door for Ty. "Thanks," Ty said, dumping everything he had onto the nearest table. Trace noticed tufts of gray hair poking out of the gym bag and could only hope that it was part of Ty's Alexander Graham Bell costume. He could wear an orange wig, flip-flops, and a tuxedo and Trace doubted that anyone here knew enough or cared enough to question whether or not he had nailed the Alexander Graham Bell look. "Okay if we meet at this table?" Ty asked.

Trace just nodded, surprised that he was even being spoken to. "So, since you were, like, sick Wednesday or whatever," Ty said dismissively, "we just need to check and make sure you actually are ready. We all know what *we're* doing," he added pointedly.

Trace breathed in slowly, anchoring himself on the back of a chair and trying to swallow the lump in his throat. The clamminess was fading. Across the table,

Ty frowned up at him, arms crossed, trying to look hard and in charge. Ms. Levy had rolled her cart to the far side of the media room and was gathering up piles of books that had been scattered across tables there.

"Look, Ty," Trace began, "I wanted to explain to you about what happened at the . . . at the library." He didn't wait for Ty to shut him down. "I was there, you know. In fact, I got there early. But I ran into a problem and these library guards, like, arrested me practically." Ty punched a straw into his juice box and chewed on it, his eyes losing some of their steel. He was listening.

"They took my phone so I couldn't even call you," Trace continued. Ty's head nodded slowly as Trace described being interrogated by the guards and about Auntie Lea being called.

"They called your aunt?" Ty looked confused. "That's harsh, man. But why? Why'd they grab you? I mean, what did you do to get on their radar in the first place?"

Trace chewed on his lip. With world-class stupidity, he had led himself right back to that kid. Before he could answer, though, the media center door burst open and Abe Lincoln clattered in, lugging nearly as many bundles as Ty had. Behind her came a silent, scowling, and empty-handed Kali.

"Let's do this," Kali said, dropping into a seat next to Ty and looking at no one. "I have places to be."

Presley dropped her book bag on the floor, hung a shopping bag on the back of a chair, and gently propped what looked like a pyramid made out of pipe cleaners and newspaper on the table. "*Kirlian* photography experiment," she announced, beaming with pride. No one asked.

"All right, just so we're all on the same page," Ty said authoritatively. Without pausing, he went over the order in which they would speak on Monday, asking each of them to tick off the topics they would cover. "Have you timed your presentation?" he asked, turning to Trace. Kali drummed her multicolored fingernails on the tabletop loudly.

Trace nodded, but Ty had moved on. "We don't need to rehearse since those of us who were here did that on Wednesday, but make sure you can do yours in three minutes, okay?"

Trace leaned back in the chair he had taken across from Ty, his hand resting on the rattle in his pocket.

"I'm good," was all he said. He was *very* good. If he showed the toy to them, they would be surprised, probably impressed, even if it would kill them to admit it. This was a genuine Civil War artifact. But no *way* would he give Kali a chance to dig up something over the weekend that might top it.

"Okay, then." Ty looked around the table at everyone and nodded. "We're ready. Anything else?" Ty had clearly taken charge of the team. Kali pushed her chair back with a screech, flipped her braids away from her shoulder, and stood.

"Oh yeah," Trace said. If not friendly, Ty seemed less hostile now, and Auntie Lea would surely question Trace when he got home—so why not? "My aunt asked me to invite you guys to a, um, Halloween party tomorrow night." That had sounded pretty corny, but Trace had decided that he couldn't care less if they came or not. "She said you can bring someone if you want and—"

"Gee, whiz! Will there be candy, and maybe we can paint our faces? Ooooooh, golly, that sounds like super fun!" Kali gushed, batting her eyelashes. "When I was *six*, maybe," she added. Pushing in her chair, Kali zipped up her jacket and gave Trace an overly sweet smile. "Monday, guys," she said flatly, heading for the door.

"—and she says that group the Vacationers is coming," Trace finished, looking from Ty to Presley. "Either of you guys wanna come?"

Presley's face blossomed into a smile so broad that it threatened to dislodge her eyebrows, which had taken a beating during the day. "Definitely. Assuredly. Indubitably. Affirmative!" she chirped.

"Wait a minute," Kali said, whipping around. "*THE* Vacationers? What are you talking about? The *Vacationer* Vacationers, as in 'Rocket' and 'Gotta Drop It' Vacationers? No *way*!" She was back in a flash, both hands flat on the table, leaning toward Trace and studying him with narrowed eyes.

*Well, well, well. Isn't this sweet?* Trace thought. "So, whaddya think, Ty?" he asked, ignoring Kali. "Auntie Lea said to invite you and Presley and anyone else I *liked*." He knew that last bit was mean, but Kali deserved it. She had pulled out a chair and was sitting down now, staring at him.

"How would someone like you even know those

guys?" she asked suspiciously. "They're like . . ." She shook her head. "Like *major*. I couldn't even get tickets to their concert next month; they were totally sold out."

"Excuse me, guys," Ms. Levy interrupted, leaning over Trace's shoulder. "I'm closing up in five minutes, okay? Anyway, shouldn't you all be in a hurry to get outta here on a Friday? For cryin' out loud, quit working!"

"Sure thing, Ms. Levy," Trace said too merrily. Kali's *someone like you* had stung, and having something she really wanted, something he could dangle in front of her nose, felt pretty good. He wondered how long he could make her squirm. Ignoring her completely, he turned his full attention on Ty and Presley. "You guys know where I live, so maybe like seven p.m.? And Auntie Lea said she'll make sure you get home safely."

"A Halloween dance party?" Presley's eyes were huge and Ty looked like he was trying hard not to grin. "Let me get this straight: The Vacationers are coming to *your* place for Halloween?" Kali said. "For real?"

Trace turned to look at her. Even with suspicion and disbelief written all over it, her face was breathtaking when he looked at her straight on. After everything she had done to make him feel small, to make it clear that he wasn't worth a moment of her time, he was surprised to see that she looked worried too. Worried that *he* might not include *her* in the invitation.

"Yes," he said finally. "The real Vacationers. Tomorrow. My house. What? Did you want to come?"

Trace was surprised, and then again, he wasn't, to see a witch chained to the iron fence in front of 810 Vanderbilt Avenue. Up close, he could see streaks in the lime-green paint on the mannequin's face and he recognized the moth-eaten shawl around her neck as one from a bag that lived by the front door, eternally destined for the Salvation Army. Auntie Lea's blue plastic-wrapped bike chain was around the witch's waist. She might be tacky, she was certainly hideous, but this was Brooklyn, and someone would haul her off if she weren't locked down.

He took the stairs two at a time. Inside, the hallway was bathed in a deep-orange glow. Auntie Lea had been busy. Strains of "Thriller" streamed from the kitchen as Michael Jackson's voice crooned,

"*Something evil's lurking in the dark. Under the moon-light . . .*" Something smelled very pumpkin-y. Trace smiled. He quietly hung his coat in the hall and waited patiently until Jackson reached the line "*You hear the door slam . . .*" And he slammed the door shut. That was a good one. But there was no reaction.

The kitchen was empty. A timer was ticking away on the stove and Trace opened the oven door to a fragrant blast of cinnamon rising off a still doughy pumpkin pie. Dropping his book bag on the table, he grabbed a banana and took in the transformation that the kitchen had undergone since he had left for school that morning.

Strings of pumpkin lights outlined the two tall windows that overlooked the backyard. A wooden bowl sat in the center of the dark-green table, loaded with mini gourds resting on autumn leaves. Trace flicked a brick-red maple leaf lightly to see if it was real. It wasn't. Stacked up next to the bowl were a column of paper cups, a pack of paper plates covered with pictures of candy corn, and enough orange and black napkins to last for ten Halloweens.

Trace tossed the banana skin in the trash and checked the timer. The pie had nine minutes to go. If he didn't see Auntie Lea upstairs, he would come back down and pull it out after he dumped his book bag in his room. Turning to go, he noticed the board. As big as it was, he could not imagine how he had missed it. Vesper and his aunt had been busy: names and dates, notes, and even newspaper clippings had sprouted up across the diagram, which looked more like a hanging shoe rack than a family tree. Here and there, photographs had been added. Trace drew closer to study the chart. At the very top was a sepia-toned picture of a woman with her hair pulled into two thick braids. Her dress looked like it had been crisp and white, and a black shawl with tassels was draped around her shoulders. Even in the faded photo, the contrast between the high, lacy collar and her dark, serious face was striking. The long fingers of her strong hands clutched the edges of the shawl. *Melissa (Sissy) May Ransom*, Trace read. Born 1856, died 1955. Auntie Lea must have taken the picture from one of the crumbly photo albums in Aunt Frenchy's basket.

Trace suddenly became aware of the timer, ticking away. No doubt Auntie Lea would be eager to fill him in on their whole family history, but he could meet all these far-flung relatives later, like tomorrow or . . .

Trace froze. There they were. Of course they would be there. *Savannah Raymond Cumberbatch. Robsen Carter.* His parents, smiling, looked down at him from the board.

Everything he had expected, everything he had feared, the reason the box of photos in his closet had gone untouched, the guilt and the bottomless ocean of pain that he knew was waiting for him if he dared to look at their pictures—none of that happened. There was only sunlight: translucent, fleeting, late October sunlight that slanted through the windows, its honey-colored liquid filling his eyes. For an instant Trace saw *everything*, felt *everything*, understood *everything*. His hand was in his dad's hand, he was five, walking to school. A warmth spread over him and he was ten, letting his mom tuck a chenille scarf around his neck. He was seven at the beach, seagulls crying overhead, then twelve, last year, wriggling away from their embarrassing hugs to board a bus for the class trip to DC.

Far away, a buzzer buzzed. He heard his aunt; she was there in the kitchen now, and she was talking to him, he knew. Her voice, the music, the oven door and pans banging, all sound was muffled. Trace realized his eyes had filled with warm, honey-colored water. And he felt himself surrounded, immersed in the light and . . . *held*. They would always be there with him, wherever he was. Always. And wherever *they* were, he knew he would always be with them. Trace closed his eyes.

# 18

The good news was: he had had the best dream ever. It had been a flying dream, like the ones he used to have. The *where* and the *why* he had taken to the air melted away the minute Trace opened his eyes, but that wistful certainty that he had always known *how* to fly remained. Plus, he had slept straight through the night. That was definitely good news.

The bad news was: he had a date with a ghost today.

All hope that Dallas Houston had forgotten about it evaporated as Auntie Lea had gushed, over a slapdash dinner of veggie burgers and kale chips last night, that she was "*deeeee*lighted" that Dallas was giving him a private tour of the library's woodworking shop. She had looked so pleased, so clearly hopeful that the two of them would have a bonding moment, that Trace had stifled his urge to shout, "What kind of lunatic, *grown-up* nutcase goes poking into shadows looking for ghosts?" It was Halloween, for crying out loud.

But at the time, Auntie Lea had been balancing precariously on a stepladder, hanging a handful of hideously hairy plush bats from the sprinkler pipes overhead, so a sudden outburst was not a good idea. He would just let her believe the man. Let her trust a deranged *meat* eater who she was happy to let drag her only nephew into the dark and haunted, moldy book graveyard.

Trace pulled on an extra sweater and dug through the pile of clean clothes that Auntie Lea had stacked on his dresser until he found a pair of thick socks. It would be chilly today, and he imagined the library stacks would be downright icy. Just thinking about the endless shelves, how they had disappeared into shadows, made him shiver. He climbed the ladder to make up his bed, tugged the covers across it, and fought off a strong urge to crawl back underneath them. Tonight, he thought, by tonight it would all be over, he would be back here, feet on the ceiling, chilling out in his bed. It was all just a question of time, exactly like Dr. Proctor had said.

*"Good morning, starshine! The earth says hello,"* Auntie Lea sang as he entered the kitchen. Trace recognized the soundtrack of *Hair*, an old hippie musical she had seen on Broadway, as it surged from the kitchen speakers. "Morning," he mumbled, faking a smile. It occurred to Trace that he had never once seen his aunt cook without backup singers handy.

Cupcake tins half filled with batter, charred cookie sheets, and a dusty collection of candleholders covered the table. Trace grabbed a banana from the fruit bowl on the counter and watched as his aunt spooned granola over the cupcake batter. "My own invention," she said, giving him a wink. "When they're done, I'll turn 'em upside down and voilà! Mini gravestones. The granola'll be, like, the dirt and gravel underneath them. Cool, huh?" She beamed proudly.

"Extremely cool," Trace agreed, dropping two pieces of bread into the toaster. Next to it were several boxes of tall, tapered, black-and-orange-striped candles. Auntie Lea entertained at the pro level. "I'll help you out when I get home, promise," he told her. Auntie Lea just nodded along with the music.

"*Semmi gond*, my man, *semmi gond*," she said in a husky voice.

Trace waited for it.

"Zat eeees, how you are zaying? 'No prrrroblem'"— she winked—"eeeen Hungarian." Auntie Lea shrugged her shoulders. "Hey. That's as close as I could find to Transylvanian. I gotta set the mood for tonight." Finished prepping the cupcakes, she swept a handful of candleholders gently into the sink and began rinsing them in warm water, scraping off any traces of old wax. Trace buttered his toast. Auntie Lea had a *lot* of candles. Hopefully, those fire sprinklers were in good working order.

Dr. Proctor's office might not have been a popular stop on the Clinton Hill trick-or-treat map, but she did have a bowl of candy by the door just the same. Trace hung up his jacket, pulling off his gloves and shoving them into a pocket. Sifting through the doctor's bowl, he polished off three caramels and was tearing into a bag of candy corn when she called his name.

"Great costume, Theo," the doctor said as Trace stretched out on the leather couch. "I almost didn't recognize you."

It took Trace a moment to realize that the doctor was joking.

"Yeah, this is my 'pass for a normal kid' disguise." He laughed. But as quickly as he said it, he realized that it was not really funny. "I mean—"

"You know what? You *are* normal in a lot of ways, Theo." Dr. Proctor smiled at him. "Everybody you see, every single person you know? They all have some problems they have to wrestle with, twenty-four-seven, every day. We're all works in progress."

"Even doctors?" Trace asked.

"Even doctors."

Trace rested his hands on his stomach, lacing his fingers together as he studied the ceiling. Sunlight was filtering into the room through slats in the shuttered windows and thousands of tiny flecks danced in the light. What gave dust the power to fly? he wondered, remembering his dream. That sense of being suspended in the air, of being weightless, lingered. He still felt good from that dream.

"So, are you looking forward to this evening?" the doctor said cautiously. "Going out with any friends?"

The thought of knocking on doors, carrying a

plastic pumpkin and scoring piles of candy, made Trace laugh. And suddenly, he found he was describing Auntie Lea's gala plans in full detail, cupcakes to candles. He re-created the kitchen for the doctor: bats hanging overhead, pumpkin lights around the window, even Auntie Lea's ancestral tree chart. The family tree. Trace caught his breath.

"Sounds like quite a project, Theo. And did you add a picture of yourself to the chart?" Dr. Proctor's voice had softened. It seemed like it was almost tiptoeing across her desk toward him.

Trace had realized too late that he had been here before with her, being led down a corridor by innocent questions only to find that a door had clicked shut behind him. He never felt himself being steered, never intentionally opened the door in the first place, but he also never seemed to see it coming. He had not helped Auntie Lea with that project at all, had changed the subject if she even brought it up. But all right, he decided. Today, for one day only, the Halloween special: anything and everything the doctor wanted him to talk about was okay. Trace studied the doctor's moonlike face as she watched him and nodded at her.

"I will. Sure," he replied evenly. "It's my family and I'm the last leaf on the tree."

An image of the bathtub in his grandmother's house suddenly popped into his head: the weird, paw-like feet that supported it, the scuffs and scratches written into the porcelain, and the rubber stopper on a chain that plugged the drain. This was how he felt now: like he was in that tub tugging away at the plug. If he just kept pulling, he would yank that stopper out and let all the murky, hot, sudsy water, and everything he needed to scrub off, just swirl away.

Then he was telling Dr. Proctor about the iPod and about the last hugs all around and then about the deer. The deer that would not have been there half an hour, or even ten minutes, earlier. Trace felt as if he dared not stop, as if this was his one chance to confess: he told her about the river, about his mom's face, her lips moving, and about his dad's kicking. He told her about the strong dark hands pulling him out, he could *see* them clearly now, and about the closed windows—but how *could* they be closed? He felt raw now, reluctant to push on that bruised spot in his chest. But this was it. He even told her the final, impossible, and unfair fact:

he was alive when all of it had been his fault.

"Or not," Dr. Proctor said simply.

Trace sat up. His face was wet. No way had he been crying.

"Wh . . . wh . . . what?"

"Things happen no matter what we do, don't they? That deer might have crossed that same road the same way a half hour earlier," Dr. Proctor said quietly. "What happened wasn't your fault."

"But I made them go back. We wouldn't have been there if . . . if . . ." Trace shook his head. That deer would *not* have been there earlier. This was some therapist mumbo jumbo she was trying to pull.

"If you had all left earlier, if you had spent the night and left the next day, if you had stopped to gas up, if your dad had driven slower or faster, or your grandmother had convinced you to stay for dinner . . . There may be a thousand what-ifs, Theo." The doctor leaned back in her chair and looked at him with a sad smile. "Why pick the one that hurts the most?" she asked.

The room was silent. Trace braced for the wave, the lump, the sick feeling that came with any thought of the accident. But the river didn't come for him. Dust motes kept dancing in the light. The doctor's clock began chiming softly.

*Good question*, he thought.

Along some blocks, the sidewalks were ankle-deep with yellow leaves. Trace had to dodge hordes of candy-craving kids, moving gang-like from store to store, as he headed for the subway. Halloween was clearly an all-day event in Brooklyn, and shopkeepers were doing their part to keep the little sugar addicts hooked and happy. On average, Trace witnessed one withdrawal tantrum per block as he sidestepped min-iature pirates, aliens, and superheroes.

Once he was settled on the train, the show contin-ued. The cast was older, the costumes more elaborate: a human iPhone leaned against the doors, President Obama slouched in the seat across from him. Trace appreciated the distraction. What he did *not* want to do was to think about where he was headed and what might await him there.

He had thought about asking Dr. Proctor if she believed in ghosts. Of course, he had heard stories around campfires as a kid. And he had sat through bunches of blockbuster movies with his friends back in Baltimore, laughing every time something levitated or popped out of a closet. But asking an adult about ghosts would mean admitting that he thought they really might exist. No question that Auntie Lea was a believer, even if she had never said anything. And this guy Dallas . . .

The subway car was overly warm. Trace unzipped his jacket and looked up at his image in the darkened window opposite him as the train sped toward Manhattan. The thought that he might see another face, the face of a child sitting next to him or, worse, floating above him, flashed through his mind. He shivered and looked away.

When at last the train lurched to a halt at Forty-Second Street, Trace jumped up, relieved to push into the subterranean throng of real people, flesh-and-blood bodies, as they carried him along or brushed past him. This whole ghost thing was silly. A rush of cold air as he headed up the stairs to the street cleared his head. He would get this over with quickly, just tell Dallas that he needed to head home and help Auntie Lea with the party.

Tugging his gloves out of his pocket, Trace heard a faint clattering sound as something hit the sidewalk.

What if he had not turned around? What if he had kept walking? he would think later. But he had turned. The little metal toy, the highlight of his 1860s presentation for Monday, the show-and-tell treasure he had forgotten was still in his pocket, was lying on 42nd Street, ready for any passerby to pick up or trample. Trace silently thanked the god of extra credit as he bent to scoop it up.

Taking the library steps two at a time, Trace shoved the toy back into his pocket, then patted it to be sure it was secure. At the information desk right inside the entrance, he gave his name and asked for Dallas Houston, then looked around while he waited.

It took some effort *not* to look too long at the woman behind the information desk. Her hair reminded him of spun sugar: pinkish orange, swept into high waves that seemed to float above her forehead, the whole mass shining as though it were shellacked. Her eyebrows, in two different colors, he noticed, were hand-drawn arcs that wobbled around the edges. Trace wasn't sure that she was in costume.

A loud squeak made him turn. Across the marble hall, the door to the guards' room was cracked open just enough to reveal the back of a bulky, dark-suited figure who was giving someone in the chair before him a hard time. Only last week, the poor guy in the chair had been him. All that Trace could see of the guy in trouble was a pair of twitching knees and one white-knuckled hand gripping the chair's armrest before the hulking figure turned and slammed the door shut. In the split second that took, Trace saw the hot seat was occupied by none other than Lemuel T. Spitz.

He should have felt delighted. He was wondering why he didn't when Dallas Houston appeared, grinning like the two of them were old pals.

"Thanks, Margaret," Dallas said to the cotton-candy-haired lady. "You look amazing today!"

The information lady gave Dallas a smile. At least, Trace *guessed* it was a smile: her thin red lips nearly disappeared as her mouth stretched into a straight line.

"Is she . . . ?" Trace began as they headed to the elevator.

"Margaret has her own sense of style," Dallas said, giving Trace a wink, "*every* day." Once in the elevator, Dallas inserted a key into a slot on a brass panel, gave it a quick turn, then pushed a button. Seconds later the doors opened onto the vast, shadowy underground that Trace had hoped never to see again.

"Right this way, Theo," Dallas said brightly. Ahead, rows of shelving melted into darkness, and whatever *could* be seen was dimly lit. Actually, Trace did not want to see anything at all, so he kept his eyes trained on the back of Dallas's blue denim shirt.

No wonder the guy was nuts, Trace thought. Working in this gloomy cavern, the air filled with book mold and wood-shaving dust, and cold, too—why was the air so chilly?—the smell of the earth down here, like a graveyard or something . . . would have anyone seeing ghosts. Trace nearly bumped into Dallas as the man turned abruptly and pushed open a heavy metal door.

"Welcome to my world," Dallas said cheerfully, holding it open.

It was as if Trace had stepped through a portal into an underground museum. The room was stuffed— nooks and crannies, shelves and drawers, hooks and bins everywhere—but everything seemed to fit just right. Glowing wood cabinets and shiny metal equipment nestled side by side under a mix of cool blue or warm golden puddles of light spotlighting different workstations. Every wall was covered: carved masks, travel posters, hats by the door, electrical cords over counters, gleaming rows of tools next to a rusty collection of old-fashioned ones that Trace thought couldn't possibly have any use now.

One corner of the room held a weathered leather sofa complete with patterned pillows, a throw blanket, and a book-burdened coffee table. Except for the wall behind it, which seemed to be covered with peeling wallpaper, it might have passed for a reading nook on one of those HGTV house tours that his mom used to watch. Soft jazz was playing and the scent of cinnamon hung in the air. It was cozy. And not at all what Trace had expected.

"So," Dallas said brightly, "want some hot cocoa, tea, cider?"

Trace shook his head and looked around, taking in the room slowly. "What's all that?" he asked, lifting his chin toward the tattered wall. He leaned over the couch to take a closer look.

"Pretty cool, huh?" Dallas beamed. "I'd kept them to see if they might come true, just tossed 'em in a box. Some of them really seemed to hit the nail on the head. Then, wham! One day I got the idea to paper the wall with them." He smiled at Trace. "What you're looking at is years of takeout, my man. Wherever your eye lands, there's always something there. Check it out: pick any one and I betcha it'll be relevant."

From the top of the couch to a height of about six and a half feet, predictions and lucky-number slips from Chinese fortune cookies had been stuck to the wall in not-so-precise rows. Some were fading, some were torn or grease-stained, and many just dangled from yellowed tape that was losing its grip.

"Seriously?" Trace asked. He suppressed a twinge of panic. He was underground with a madman. A madman with sharp tools and buzz saws. And ghosts. If he did manage to get out of there in one piece, if he told Auntie Lea about all of this, she'd probably just start saving fortune cookies to help the guy out. For now, Trace was just annoyed. "Look. I promised Auntie Lea I'd be back soon. So, can we please just do this . . . this, whatever it is you got me down here for?"

Dallas grinned and held up both hands. "A'ight, a'ight." Reaching around Trace, he pressed one loose fortune firmly against the wall. *"The past can be your darkness or your lamp,"* he read. "Good one. I know, I know, I gotta tape some of these down better."

Patting Trace on the shoulder, Dallas turned to pour

himself some hot cider. Lifting his mug, he offered to pour another one, but Trace shook his head; he hadn't even noticed the mini kitchen tucked into the shelving near the couch. A melancholy John Coltrane number drifted out of the iPad that was propped atop a microwave oven. It was a tune his dad used to play, and Trace could feel the music wash through him, familiar and warm—*tender* was how his dad had described it. "In a Sentimental Mood."

Dallas gestured for him to sit on the couch, but when Trace remained standing, he pulled a stool out from under a worktable with his foot and sat down, mug in hand, in no apparent hurry. He took a hesitant sip, set the mug down, and studied Trace.

"Look, man, I didn't really think we'd go do a ghost-hunter thing. I just thought it would be cool to talk. I really like your Auntie Lea and I felt, well . . . I wanted to get to know you a bit and for you to get to know me too, all right? I mean, I hope to be spending some time with her and, hey, man to man, I just want us to be cool, that's all." Dallas took a deep breath, leaned back, and crossed his arms, waiting.

Trace knew the ball was in his court. He figured he should give the man a hard time. Put him through a workout, grill him for some history, or make him prove somehow that he was worthy of Auntie Lea's attention. That he had anything to say about what his aunt did or didn't do was news to him. But it was kind of nice that Dallas had asked. Trace smiled.

"If Auntie Lea's cool with you, that's what counts. We're good, man," he said. "So, this isn't about that whole thing with the guards and the kid?"

"That business upstairs with Spitz?" Dallas shook his head. "He probably watches too many cops and robbers shows, you know? The library's kinda short on criminal activity and he musta figured he'd hit the big time with you. Let's just say Spitz has, um, missed a few software updates, you know?" Dallas took a slow sip of his cider.

"Okay," he continued when Trace said nothing. "So the ghost thing."

Trace braced himself.

"I can't say I've actually *seen* anyone. I think I see something, someone, and then when I turn or when I get closer, it's a stack of boxes or a chair that's been covered. I thought I saw a kid one time, though, I really did." Dallas seemed focused on a space above Trace's head, as though trying to pull the memory out of the ether.

He nodded slowly, like he needed to reassure himself. "There is definitely a vibe that's out there," he said, gesturing toward the door, which Trace was very happy to see had been closed behind them. "I guess I stretched that bit about actually *seeing* anyone. But I do hear things from time to time. Things that, well, I chalk up for the most part to creaky shelves, or the building's old and stuff is settling, or maybe it's just cranky pipes—that sorta thing. But when I heard Spitz giving you the third degree I thought maybe you had seen him. You saw a kid, right?"

Trace exhaled, not even aware that he had been holding his breath. He really wanted to be done with this. "Right," he said. "Just like I told the guards." If he kept it short and sweet, maybe they could just leave.

"You know, this building—well, this property anyway—has some history to it. I don't know if you know this, but—" Dallas began.

"Yeah, the draft riots, the orphanage fire in 1863, I know," Trace said, more curtly than he had intended. "Got it."

"Whoa." Dallas leaned back, took up his mug again. "A historian. So maybe it's not just my imagination at all; maybe it's leftover energy or an aura or whatever—but nothing scary, okay? 'Cause nobody died or anything, they just—"

"A kid *was* killed," Trace interjected, immediately sorry he had said it. "I mean, some sources say that and some don't, so . . . so it's just that I've been doing research for a school project and we've . . . well, I've been reading, that's all." Dallas was leaning forward now, giving him a puzzled look and nodding for him to go on.

"There was a girl, a nine-year-old girl who . . . who didn't get out. I read that a crowd of angry white folks found her and . . ." Trace's voice unintentionally dropped to a whisper. "And they beat her to death. That's what some sources say anyway," he added quickly. The air around them was swirling with the last strains of Coltrane's ballad, and then there was silence.

Suddenly a marimba beat erupted from Dallas's shirt pocket, making them both jump. He fumbled for his phone.

"Houston speaking," he said briskly. "Right. Can you bring it down? Okay, okay. What room? Gimme five minutes, ten maybe." He pocketed the phone.

"Look, I have to go pick up a bench real quick. Tell you what. You chill here for a minute and, when I get back, we'll head on over to Lea's and help her set up for the party, okay? I'm taking off early today. We'll see what we can see between here and the elevator and that'll be it, deal? You're officially off the hook." Smiling, Dallas offered his hand to shake.

Trace grinned. Fortune cookie collection aside, the guy wasn't entirely nuts. He shook Dallas's hand.

"Do you need help carrying the bench?" Trace asked.

"No, thanks. Probably against union rules anyway, if not child labor laws," Dallas said with a wink. "Do me a favor and polish off that cider though. There's a mug on the shelf there and a jar of cinnamon sticks. I'll be right back."

Another tune came on. A Miles Davis piece called "So What" that Trace remembered, another of his dad's favorites. He would have to find some of those songs and download them. Pouring himself what remained of the cider, he dropped a cinnamon stick into it and sank onto the couch. All the books on the coffee table, he noticed, featured wood, in one form or another. There was one about covered bridges and another about trees, with a deer on the cover stepping gingerly out of a dense forest. Damn deer. Trace eased out of his jacket, twisting to bunch it up by his side on the couch. With a clatter, the toy rattle fell from the pocket again. Trace retrieved it and rested it on the coffee table. He would have to be more careful.

Very quietly, something nearby shifted. There was a soft shuffling sound, then an intake of air like a sob. Trace froze, hearing every note that Miles was draining from his trumpet. Was it the music? A scratch in the recording?

"Sissy," said a small voice.

It was coming from inside the room.

19

So.

A direct lightning strike. Jamming your finger into an electrical socket. Maybe seeing an alien at the foot of your bed. Whatever scenarios Trace might later think would describe this moment would miss the mark. Thinking, in fact, had not been an option.

But his body had reacted. He could feel the hair on his arms standing on end, wavering as though caught in an electrical current. And suddenly he was lifted, yanked up and left floating somewhere near the top of the room, just long enough to look down at himself frozen on the couch. Then, with a crackle, he snapped back into his body: that was how it felt, like he had just arrived in his skin. He couldn't move; only his eyes seemed to work, so he blinked them rapidly, trying to reboot his brain.

The little boy was standing just inside the door, the *closed* door, and he was real. Trace was sure of it. The tattered clothes, the ripped-up shoes, the huge eyes watching him: the boy could not be a ghost. He was the clearest, *realest*, most sharply defined thing in the room. But everything around him, the hard wood shelves, the steel equipment, lamps, books, and, to his amazement, even his own hands when he looked down at them, seemed faded and fuzzy-edged now. It was as though nothing else was real *except* the boy. Trace stared, mouth open, wanting to say something.

"Sissy!" said the boy again, more emphatically.

Trace shook his head hard and all the scared melted away. The kid had called him a sissy?

"Hey, watch it, little man. I don't know where you're from, but calling people—"

"Where Sissy?" the boy said again. "When Sissy comin'?" The boy looked smaller than Trace remembered; the little fingers poking out of his ratty shirtsleeves were tiny and soft and, even from where he sat,

Trace could see they were nicked with dozens of scars.

"W . . . w . . . when Sissy comin'?" the boy repeated mournfully. Pale tear tracks ran down his dark cheeks; his face crumpled. The kid was going to wail.

"Hey, hey, hey," Trace said, leaning forward. "*Sissy*—is that your sister? She brought you here? You want to go find her?" He was *not* going through this again. Where was Dallas? Let him deal with this; let Dallas figure out if this kid was real. The boy had begun sniffling, all trembling lips and sucked-in sobs. A full-scale meltdown was in progress.

"Look, it's okay. We're gonna find your sister, okay?" Trace said gently. As he stood up, the boy lurched backward against the wall, so he moved no closer.

"Sissy comin'?" Trace met the boy's eyes and he felt his heart break. The kid looked *so* frightened and *so* alone. Maybe she was in the library, he thought. Maybe they could find her. For a moment, Trace hoped the sister would be old enough for him to smack upside the head. "What's your name, little man?"

The boy didn't answer, just stared at him, clearly scared out of his wits. Where was Dallas? Trace looked around the room, searching for something, anything, to calm the kid down. Maybe hot chocolate or apple cider? But what if the kid had some freaky food allergy? His eyes landed on the metal rattle.

"Cholly," the boy said softly. "I'se Cholly. Sissy said wait."

"Oh, cool!" Trace said, giving the boy a big smile. The kid had calmed down. Picking up the toy, he took a cautious step in the boy's direction. "I'm Trace. Trace Carter, okay? I'm going to help you find your sister."

Trace moved slowly, smiling and nodding his head slightly with every step. The boy watched him carefully.

"They gone. They all gone. Sissy said wait," the boy repeated.

Trace squatted down when he was at arm's length from the boy. They were face-to-face. This was a real boy. How he had gotten in, where he had been hiding since last week . . . none of that mattered at the moment.

"Well," Trace said gently, "when my friend comes back, we'll go look for her upstairs, all right?"

"No!" Cholly yelled. A floodgate had opened. "No! They gone! We gotta go! Sissy gonna get my—" The boy froze, staring at the rattle in Trace's hands.

"Sissy?" The boy's eyes moved from the rattle to Trace and back. Trace had no idea how to answer the boy. So he simply handed Cholly the rattle. The boy turned the toy over in his hands, gave it a little shake, and then settled his large dark eyes on Trace again. All the fretfulness had melted away and his face softened into a smile.

Good. Now they could just chill till Dallas turned up, Trace was thinking. But suddenly, the boy looked frantically at the door, then ran to tuck himself under a shelf in the corner of the room. He crouched, making himself a little ball huddled around the rattle in his hands.

"Hide," he rasped hoarsely.

*What now?* Trace thought, getting to his feet. "Look, stay here, Cholly. I'm gonna get somebody who'll help us out, okay? You just sit tight and I'll be right back."

"Hide," the boy said again. "Fire!"

Unbelievable. The kid was getting panicky again. Trace took a second to think about the consequences of leaving a child in a room full of dangerous tools, then decided to take the chance. He wished he had gotten Dallas's phone number. Let him deal with this.

"Stay here," he said to the boy, trying to sound authoritative.

Trace smelled smoke before he saw it, seeping in deadly white curls underneath the door. There really was fire. His heart began hammering in his throat as his brain threw him right back to sixth grade: fourth row on the aisle in the Hamilton Middle School auditorium, doodling while Fireman Jack listed his top do's and don'ts of fire prevention. Should he block the smoke with something?

Trace scanned the room. A couple of dish towels hung from a hook near the hot plate. They would do. He grabbed them both. But if he blocked them into the room, what if the fire trapped them here? The boy was whimpering in the corner, starting to cry.

"It's okay, it's okay," Trace said, hoping he sounded calmer than he felt.

"I think we should leave," he added hesitantly. He was not at all sure what Fireman Jack had said about opening doors. Put your hand on it, see if it's hot. That's right. Trace was sweating now. Even though the room had warmed up, it wasn't that hot. But it was getting too smoky. He'd look, then he'd grab the kid and make a run for it. Trace placed his hand on the door.

"Yeowwch!" he cried, jerking his hand away from the hot metal. They were trapped! Wrapping the towels around his hand, Trace's instincts kicked in: better to run for it than to stay and burn. He grabbed the knob and yanked open the door.

"Hey, thanks, man," Dallas said, pushing into the room with his shoulder. He held a small wooden bench against his hip. "This'll only take a second, then we're out, okay?"

Trace stood stock-still as Dallas placed the bench in the center of the room, next to a couple of metal stools. He could see enough of the vast underground library beyond the door to know: there was no fire. No smoke. Only a chilly dampness hung in the air. Slowly, his pulse thumping so crazily that he felt dizzy, Trace turned toward Cholly, dreading what he already knew he would see: nothing.

"Hey, man, you all right?" Dallas asked, studying him with alarm.

A gasping, smoky *NO* tried to force its way out of Trace's throat, hogging all the air in his lungs. The ground was getting wobbly and he felt his knees buckle.

*Strange, how close to flying this feels*, Trace thought. And then he landed. He was on the couch and Dallas Houston was fanning his face with a magazine. The breeze was cooling his sweaty face and Trace breathed it in, watching as some of it sailed upward to set the Chinese fortunes rippling.

# 20

Trace could count on one finger the times he had been in a New York City cab. That first and only ride, the one from LaGuardia Airport with Auntie Lea after his parents' funeral, had been a bumpy, careening dash, streetlights and exit signs streaking past dark windows. This one promised quiet, and Trace leaned his head gratefully against the leather seat and closed his eyes.

Dallas Houston had said very little and asked nothing. He had simply picked up the phone on his desk and called Auntie Lea, not a trace of worry in his voice, to ask if she needed anything for the party. They were on the way, he had said. They might make a stop or two, but they would be there in a couple of hours at the most. And when Trace's head had stopped throbbing and he had sat up, Dallas helped him into his jacket and gently steered him out of the stacks, upstairs and across the lobby, then out onto Fifth Avenue. Only a few tourists and shivering teenagers remained huddled stubbornly on the cold steps.

A black town car was waiting for them at the curb and Trace had slid in when Dallas opened the door, no questions asked. Traffic was at a crawl on Fifth Avenue. It was, after all, Saturday afternoon, Halloween, midtown Manhattan. But the honking and braking and yelling outside the car were reduced to a muffled hum beneath the soft melody flowing from the speakers. Only when Trace stuck his hands in his jacket pockets did he think of the rattle. That it was gone for good, he felt certain. He could see the floor, the shelves, the corner of the workshop clearly in his mind. The emptiness where the boy had been crouched had been complete. The rattle was gone. *Where* it had gone or *how* . . . Trace needed to think about later, when thinking might be a possibility.

After a blissfully smooth ride, the driver pulled

over to the curb on Myrtle Avenue. Dallas climbed out and Trace, feeling like his body was on autopilot, followed. They were still a couple of blocks away from Vanderbilt, but he was in no hurry to switch gears and pretend to be in party mode. So when Dallas held open the door to Mel's Diner, a dark, old-timey-looking place that Trace had never noticed before, he went with the program, followed the waiter who greeted them, and slid into the booth Dallas chose.

Trace was well aware that his brains had been sucked clean. And that was okay. As calmly as if it were a tabloid headline he was reading on line at the grocery store, the words *You're crazy* floated into his mind. Followed by *Nuts, Bonkers* . . . and then *Chemical imbalance*. He had heard that phrase on a TV show and, because it was oddly comforting, he let it bounce around in his head for a minute. Dallas was talking to a waiter and sneaking worried glances his way, but Trace was rummaging through other words . . . through stories he had heard about losing your mind. *Twinkle . . . Winky . . . Tinkle . . .* what was the phrase? The *Twinkie Defense*, that was it. He read once that eating too much sugar supposedly had made some guy somewhere kill somebody or something. Trace shook his head. Who knew? Maybe he had been just one Snickers away from completely insane all this time.

A plate clattered to the table in front of him.

"Let's talk," Dallas said, smiling at him slightly and reaching for the ketchup bottle.

Trace looked up. It was a good thing that Dallas was all the way across the table, because the smell of hamburger and french fries made him want to hug the man. He was *starving*. But hugging would have been seriously uncool. Since coming to live with Auntie Lea, hamburger had become an exotic delicacy; the version served in the school cafeteria, scooped from vats Ty swore were labeled *BEEF: Grade D, but edible*, gave off no smell at all. Scary stuff.

"So," Dallas began.

"Hmmmph." Trace nodded, his mouth stuffed with fries. Talking was a great idea. Brilliant. Because right now, squirting mustard in a spiral atop his burger, he felt thankful. Thankful that somebody, *any*body, might please, please, please sort this out. Maybe Dallas could tell him what parts were real—and what things could not possibly be.

"Clearly something happened while I was gone, Theo," Dallas began. "When I came in you were sweating and standing there like you'd seen a . . . well, like you'd seen, you know . . ." Dallas waited.

Trace took a big swig of the lemonade Dallas had ordered for him. The curious feeling that he was observing this moment, but from somewhere inside of himself and only as an interested bystander, was hard to shake. He really needed some answers. "I saw the boy. I don't know how he got in the room. I mean, I never opened the door or anything, but there he was, crying again." Trace sipped his lemonade. "Crazy, right? He couldn't be there. But he was. Clear as I'm looking at you." Boy did this sound nuts. "Oh, and he spoke this time."

Dallas cocked his head, his hand frozen halfway to his mouth holding the last corner of his burger. "He talked to you?"

Trace nodded. "He kept asking for someone named Sissy. I guess that was his sister? Oh, and he told me his name." Trace sat up, excited. "Cholly. That's something, right? I mean, if we did some research? Maybe there was a Cholly in the orphanage and—"

"Whoa," Dallas broke in. "*If* it was a ghost—and believe me, I'm open to that—and *if* he was looking for his sister, well then, he might not have been an orphan at all, see what I mean? That kid might've gotten separated from his family, right?" Dallas leaned toward him, brows furrowed over his dark eyes. "I know you're doing that report on the draft riots, Theo, but you're connecting some pretty loose dots."

"The kid said 'hide,'" Trace went on, sure of himself. "And he said 'fire.'"

"I smelled the smoke, Dallas. I saw it coming in under the door." Trace felt himself settle back into his skin, aware that remnants of the panic he had felt earlier were waiting for him. He looked Dallas straight in the eyes. "There *was* a fire. I burned my hand on your door."

Dallas leaned back, crossed his arms over his chest, and studied a spot near the ceiling for a minute. "I did smell something," he finally said. "I've smelled it before. Faint, though. Smoky. Like burning trash." He raised his chin toward the front of the restaurant, then signed the air with his hand, the universal signal for the waiter to bring the check.

"From time to time, there's a burning smell. Down

there, with all those old books, as dank as it is, I just chalk it up to odors being released when it rains, or drafts getting in if anyone opens a door, you know? First coupla times, I went scouting around, thinking there might really be a fire. But after a while, you just get used to things." Dallas had a dreamy look on his face. "But I know there are ghosts, man. And this one? This one seemed to be waiting for—"

"Get you guys anything else?" the waiter broke in. Dallas shook his head, handed him a credit card, and sent him on his way.

"Waiting for Sissy—whoever *she* was, right?" Trace said. Talking to Dallas was cool. If an adult thought this was real, maybe he wasn't going crazy.

"Maybe. But I was gonna say waiting for *you*, Theo." Trace blinked.

"Why do I get the feeling that you haven't told me everything?" Dallas asked, scooting out from the booth and slipping into his jacket.

Trace polished off a last fry, wiped his mouth, and grabbed his jacket too. Why shouldn't he? Maybe the rattle had moved somehow, maybe it was still down there in his workshop. Besides, Dallas believed him already; he hadn't tried to convince him that the kid must be an invention of his imagination. And neither was that rattle. Auntie Lea had seen it. Roman, Angel, and Presley had, too. *Presley*. The rattle had actually burned her!

Dallas was waiting for him at the cash register. "Wanna finish the story?" he asked.

So Trace did.

# 21

In the short time that it had taken to pick up sodas and chips and walk home, Trace had told Dallas everything he knew about the rattle. It would no longer be the showpiece for his presentation on Monday, but that seemed okay somehow. The boy had looked so happy, so relieved in that moment when he took the rattle, that it seemed like the toy had been put to a much better use. It felt good too that Dallas had listened carefully, like he was slipping this bit of information into a puzzle that he and Trace were trying to solve together.

Twilight had helped set the stage for Halloween, casting long violet shadows across streets and darkening the doorways they passed. Along Vanderbilt Avenue, pumpkins glowed in windows, cobwebs undulated in doorways, and, even from half a block away, Trace could tell that the witch in front of number 810 had been further accessorized. Her splotchy green face was now bathed in a light from below that blinked on and off periodically. He had to give Auntie Lea kudos: it would probably freak out a few little kids whenever the hideous face suddenly lit up.

Inside the apartment, diaphanous scarves had been draped over the hallway lights and a fan was rigged up over the stairs to keep them gently blowing. The shifting patterns of orange light that they created really did feel otherworldly. Trace heard a curious droning sound coming from the front room as he entered the apartment, then a sudden burst of laughter erupted in the kitchen at the end of the hallway. That laugh could only be Dawoud's, he thought. An immediate "*Just HUSH*" followed. Brenda, no doubt . . . which confirmed his suspicion: the Cuties were in the house.

"All *ri-i-ight*," Dallas drawled. He had emerged from the kitchen and joined Trace as he was inspecting the room's transformation. "Your aunt does not party lightly, I see."

Trace surveyed Auntie Lea's conversion of the room since that morning. It was now party central, with two mikes and a keyboard standing in front of the bay window, a guitar propped up against Auntie Lea's bookcase, and an assortment of handheld instruments stacked on her armchair. An amp at the foot of her wide couch, which was now pillow-lined and free of the magazines that had littered it earlier, hummed menacingly. Auntie Lea's treasured Moroccan carpet had completely disappeared. Trace grinned. Watching old folks dance was going to be pretty entertaining.

He had seen the Vacationers repeatedly on VH1, then once as musical guests on a *Saturday Night Live* episode, and last summer performing on the BET Awards. Finding two of them bent over the kitchen table, dressed in shiny metallic silver jumpsuits and sporting humongous Afro wigs, should have blown him away. But meeting a hundred-and-fifty-year-old ghost up close and personal was probably as much shock as he could process for one day. So Trace simply nodded their way and began unpacking the bags of chips he had been carrying.

"Theo . . . um, I mean, Trace, my man," Dawoud said with a wink. "Your aunt's getting dressed; she'll be down in a minute." He gave Dallas a pat on the back, and, based on the kiss Dallas planted on Brenda's cheek, Trace realized that they had all met already.

"Meet my nephews," Dawoud continued. "*I* can call 'em Terrence and Jerome 'cause *I* changed their diapers. But the last time someone called 'em Terry and Jerry we needed bandages and a fire extinguisher, so let me introduce you to Mr. Big Time Trax over there on frosting and his pardner, the Infamous Jinx, on engraving." Dawoud turned back to the pots on the stove, his shoulders shaking and his head bobbing. He had clearly cracked himself up, but his twin nephews merely sighed.

The two multiplatinum recording artists stopped what they were doing, got up to shake Trace's hand, and rolled their eyes in the direction of their uncle. Then they returned to slathering gray icing and writing cryptic messages on Auntie Lea's gravestone cupcakes. Trace shook his head. If he snapped a picture of this scene, it would break Instagram.

"Good to meet you guys," was all he said. "I'm gonna go get . . . um, get ready for . . . uh . . ." Trace trailed off. It wasn't like he had a costume. But he could definitely use a minute alone in his room. He still felt pretty weird. Strange. Or what would Presley call it? Pixified? Discombobulated? Rattled? Trace took the stairs to his room two at a time. Any word but *rattle*.

Maybe he should pull together a costume—at least make it look like he was trying to—Trace stopped cold. Celeste, the petite lead singer of the Vacationers, was leaning over Auntie Lea's table, strings of beads in her hand, her massive pink Afro framed by a halo of golden light that poured through the bedroom window. Her silver jumpsuit was catching and throwing off flashes of the Technicolor sunset as it unfolded behind her.

Of *course* there were three of them. Of *course* he knew that she was part of the group. But he had totally forgotten about her. Clearly, the sight of two celebrities decorating cupcakes in his aunt's kitchen was as much as his brain had been able to absorb.

"'Ello, sweetness," the girl purred. "I am Celeste, yes? And you are?" Trace swallowed. Okay. He knew that Trax and Jinx had met her on a vacation in Martinique. He knew that she was the lead vocalist on their song "Rocket." He even knew from *E! News* that her first movie, a sci-fi thriller called *Qasar*, was opening next month. But what *was* his name?

Celeste studied him, an easy smile spreading across her face. Wobbling slightly on a pair of silver platform heels, she came over to Trace and delivered three kisses to his cheeks: left, right, and left again. The silver jumpsuit, Trace noticed, definitely looked better on her than on Trax and Jinx.

"I, uh, I'm . . . ," he mumbled. His room was an unholy mess. He had never cleaned up after knocking over Aunt Frenchy's basket. The bedcovers were sloppily pulled across his bed and his desk was littered with the books and index cards he had been using for his report. The room smelled like old socks and mustard. Not good. Trace glared at Aunt Frenchy's basket and the strings of beads that Auntie Lea had left all over the table. The girl must think he was a total slob.

"Oh, hey, no," Celeste said quickly, catching his eye. "Ees okay. Your aunt, she says I can borrow zees jewelry for my costume, yes? You are zinking zat I am a zief?" The girl grinned slyly.

"T . . . Tr . . . Trace," he coughed out, hoping that what he was actually thinking was not written all over his face. "Um, that's my name," he added. "And, no, no, no . . . I wasn't *zinking* . . . uh, thinking anything like that." Trace gave her a smile that he hoped looked charming and confident.

"Ah, well, I leave you now, okay?" Celeste carefully lifted strands of silver and green glass beads that she had chosen over her gigantic wig. "*Pli ta*, sweetness," she crooned. "See you later . . . *meester* Trace." She blew him a kiss, then closed the door gently behind her.

Trace had wanted privacy. But while he couldn't put his finger on just what the difference was, after Celeste left, his room felt more empty than private. Being alone usually made him feel stronger and more solid. He was wondering why it now felt like something had gone missing when he noticed that Aunt Frenchy's basket had been thoroughly picked through; her things were spread all over the table.

Trace collected photo albums that were still on the floor and scooped up handkerchiefs and a fan from the table. None of this stuff would work for any costume that he would ever wear. Shoving everything into the basket, he noticed a corner of folded paper peeking out of a pocket sewn into the lining. He had never rummaged through the basket, had never been the least bit curious about its contents until now. The paper was yellowed and, though folded, thin enough to reveal that there was handwriting on it.

Gingerly, he slipped the paper out and carefully unfolded it. Creases darkened with dust and age crisscrossed the fragile page, and the ink had faded in places. *Dearest Charles*, it began.

Trace paused. It looked like a love letter: too private and too personal. Reading it would be like sneaking a peek into someone's diary, and that seemed wrong. He would simply fold it up, put it back in the pocket, and tell Auntie Lea about it later. And he meant to. But something at the bottom of the page caught his eye: a pair of pale, ragged-edged splotches, teardrops that had all but washed away the words written there. Trace read what remained: *F_ rgive me, your Me _ iss_* .

Carefully folding the letter, he returned it to the basket. Downstairs, a bass line began thumping and Celeste's voice came floating up the stairs as she tested the microphone. Trace was making a halfhearted effort to find something, *anything*, that might work as a costume when there was a soft knock at his door.

"Uhhhhh, lemme guess," he said, swinging the door open. Good thing that Presley had warned him. "Mr. Alexander Graham Bell, inventor of the telephone, I believe?"

"And so much more," Ty added, grinning out from behind a confusion of matted gray hair. "Got a minute?" He genuinely looked as though he thought Trace might not let him in.

"Got a leash for that thing?" Trace laughed.

With one tug, Tiberius pulled off the wig, mustache, and beard he had been wearing. "My own *puh* . . . *puh* . . . creation," he said proudly, sputtering to shake off the loose hairs that were clinging to his lips. "Made it myself, all one piece, see? Fits like a ski mask."

"Brilliant," Trace conceded. "Glad you could make it, man."

Downstairs, the doorbell rang repeatedly. Auntie Lea's voice, her laughter, rang out above Celeste's random notes. The party was starting.

"Yeah, well . . . I wanted to talk to you about, well, that whole thing at the library, you know, with . . . ," Ty said, screwing up his face. He ran a hand through his spiky black hair, then scratched his chin. "That thing itches like crazy," he said, laughing.

Trace only smiled.

"So, I was pretty pissed, okay? I thought you had bailed on me. Kali went total diva the nanosecond you were late, like we had some fiendish plan to waste her Saturday. She performed. Seriously. Like she was auditioning for a reality show, man. And Little Miss Pippi Longstocking? Geesh." Ty shook his head, his shoulders shuddering at the memory.

"Do *not* go into a library with her, okay? Ever. I knew that Kali could be explosive. I mean, she might rip into anyone handy, but Presley? Geeeesh, I mean . . . that girl *hyperventilates* words." Ty looked wild-eyed, as though he was reliving being tortured by enemy combatants. "Man. I thought you were just leaving me there with those . . . those . . ." Ty trailed off. "Those *girls*."

Trace nodded. He had thought Presley had been exaggerating about that scene in the library. But now Trace really understood just how awkward and uncomfortable Ty must have felt. "What doesn't kill you makes you stronger," he could hear his dad say. Trace bit his lip, sparing Ty that piece of wisdom. *Technically*, Kali and Presley weren't killers.

"No sweat, man," he said, softly landing a punch

on Ty's shoulder. "We're cool. Those two could make Gandhi curse, you know?" Trace laughed at the thought. "But check it out . . . they may each be on their own planets, but the nanosecond you took charge, they both chilled out. Least, you *looked* like the man with the plan when we met after class." Trace studied his friend's face. "You really stepped up, man. For real."

"Yeah, well . . . ," Ty said, smiling shyly. "Gotta stick to the Prime Directive when dealing with alien life-forms, right?" He flashed Spock's hand signal for "live long and prosper." They were good.

"A'ight, then." Trace said. "Now, will you wrestle that hair-hat of yours back on, please? We've got a party to go to."

# 22

Trace's party history was pretty lightweight. He had wet his pants at his third birthday party when a clown, red-lipped with blacked-out teeth, burst into the dining room. On his tenth birthday, most of the kids he had invited went to Ollie Scheiner's party at the National Aquarium instead. Ollie had promised everyone that they would get to pet a killer whale. Even Trace had wanted to go. But his birthday cake had been ordered and his dad, clueless about what they were up against, had actually set out bowls of Goldfish for the three kids who did show up. Unless and until Ollie Scheiner left town, Trace had sworn off birthday parties. Other than that, the only parties at his house that he remembered were the ones his mom had given for her book club . . . and those were not remotely party-like.

Auntie Lea's party, Trace noted as they hit the bottom steps, was a whole other animal. A pulse seemed to be rippling through the apartment, and costumed bodies were bobbing to the music that thumped out of the front room.

*"Ya said ya loved me, ya'd never leave me . . . and I believed ya, but ya li-li-lied. Ya called me 'Baby,' ya told me maybe . . . and I believed ya, but ya li-li-lied."* Ty was grinning so widely that the edges of his beard and mustache had abandoned their position and were flapping to the beat of the music as he nodded. Trace watched in amazement as his friend turned sharply to follow his nose toward the delicious aromas coming from the kitchen. The new, take-charge Ty was singing *"You li-li-lied"* as his bobbing gray wig disappeared between a mermaid and a pharaoh.

The hallway was packed. Bathed in wavering orange light from above, the small crowd before him, in their masks and helmets, fur and feathers, took on a fairy-tale quality. The line *If you go out in the woods today, you're sure of a big surprise* popped into his mind. What was the name of that bedtime song? It had always given him chills.

Easing his way into the front room, Trace found a spot against the wall from which he could observe but stay out of the fray. "The Teddy Bear's Picnic." That was it. And it did feel like he had stumbled upon a scene in some strange woods. No dunking for apples or candy-corn-filled gift bags at this Halloween party. Auntie Lea was in a black catsuit, polka-dotted with glittery white spots that seemed to form constellations: yep, she had fit both the Big and Little Dipper across her back. She was dancing with Dallas, who still wore the faded denim shirt and pants that he'd had on earlier. Both of them sported headbands: a row of silver stars for Auntie Lea and a wobbling yellow Styrofoam ball atop Dallas's head. Trace grimaced. Was he a wounded bee? A Martian? Then it hit him: Night and Day. Got it. *Cute*.

A photographer's lamp had been hooked up to give the Vacationers a spotlight and Celeste was up on a milk crate, her pink Afro undulating with every beat of the song. She was stomping in her silver platform shoes on the tiny surface of the box like she was onstage at the Barclays Center. She looked happy. Trace felt himself smiling, nodding, and moving with the music. Celeste looked his way and—was that a wink? Trace laughed. This was crazy.

If he had to record what happened next or when or where or who did or said what, he would never be able to do it. Before his eyes, the night was blurring into a steady drone of music and voices, the air becoming liquid. The whole place was humming. One minute, he was in the kitchen with Ty, popping sweet potato fritters into his mouth and gulping orange-colored lemonade, and the next he was being pulled back toward the music by Angel. She had arrived wearing small silk wings, *of course*, and a halo that kept slipping to the side of her head. Roman came as a ninja, wearing all black and looking very mysterious. They had brought along their neighbor, Rico, who was eleven or twelve at most and claimed to be a Minion. But there was not a speck of yellow on him.

And then Trace was dancing. The floorboards seemed to dip as the entire room bounced to the music. Angel was trying to tell him something, but he couldn't hear her until she leaned in to yell, "I think Rico's in love!" Raising her hands over her head, she pumped the air and shouted out the refrain that Trax and Jinx were singing: "*Drop it! Drop it! Gotta drop it! You can't stop it, you can't top it. Better drop it.*"

Trace turned to look. Rico was grinning giddily as he spun, then tried to dip his dance partner: none other than Abe Lincoln herself. The deep plunge sent Presley's stovepipe hat soundlessly to the floor, and she scooped it up before it could get trampled. Her face was glowing and she was one eyebrow short of a pair. Trace grinned. Across the room, Ty was giggling with a tall girl dressed as a rabbit. He had ditched his wig and, as far as Trace could tell, was either having a seizure or dancing. Trace laughed out loud.

Vesper and Talia danced by, each wearing glitter in their hair and hula skirts, and each attached to guys Trace had never met. The doorbell rang periodically and new faces arrived. The room filled up, the room thinned out. Following the scent of fried chicken, Trace wove his way into the kitchen, only to interrupt a cupcake moment between Presley and Rico. He listened to them chattering away for a few minutes until she paused, looked at him like the eavesdropper he was, and said dismissively, "Oh, hello, *Trace.*"

He headed back to the music, shaking his head in wonder. Presley Jackson had not uttered one big word while talking to Rico. And now Ty was slow dancing with the rabbit. This was a weird night. And then, no encouragement needed, he was dancing again. With Brenda, with Vesper, with Brenda again. And singing! He actually heard himself singing out loud along with everyone else in the room. Possibly everyone on the block. In fact, he felt that if he threw open the front door, all of Brooklyn might be singing tonight.

Suddenly, the song ended and there were arms around his shoulders. Auntie Lea, attacking from behind, planted a kiss on his cheek. "Happy Halloween, kiddo. Having fun?" she whispered in his ear.

Trace nodded, surprised to find that he was. He really was. Everyone in the room began chanting "Rocket! Rocket! Rocket!" as if on cue. He wanted to thank Auntie Lea, to tell her how good this all was, how cool her friends were. But just as he turned toward her, his name came blasting out of the speakers.

"Trace, mon! Get on up 'ere!" Celeste commanded. Flanking her, Trax and Jinx were nodding and pointing at him. The chanting in the room changed to "Trace! Trace! Trace!" Auntie Lea gave him the gentlest of pushes and, as though he was being carried by the sound waves themselves, by the hands squeezing his shoulders and patting his back, he was propelled toward the spotlight. He knew he should be embarrassed, but he felt too good. Celeste, with the mike in one hand, swung an arm over his shoulder and gave him a kiss on the cheek. Trace turned to face the room, hamming it up a bit by shaking as though he had just been struck by a bolt of lightning.

"Meester Trace ees going to 'elp us out 'ere with zee last song of the night," Celeste crooned, pouting prettily at the crowd. Trax ran his fingers over the keyboard and the opening notes to "Rocket" detonated. Anyone who had been in the kitchen was now jockeying for a spot in the doorway. "You got zis," Celeste whispered in his ear, holding the mike so they could share it.

And then he was leaning in, cheek to cheek with Celeste, singing for all he was worth, matching her note for note, falling back when Trax and Jinx began the refrain, then leaping in to belt out, ". . . *rocket, rocket, rocket!*" It was insane. It was sweet. And Trace was pretty sure this was as cool as he would ever feel in his entire life. He looked out over the crowd and the whole room was singing. *With him*. Dallas stood behind Auntie Lea, holding her and rocking to the music. Angel was dancing with her dad, fists pumping the air. Presley and Ty and Rico were together, jumping like tadpoles and cracking themselves up.

And then it was just him and Celeste, their voices pouring out of the speakers: *"You threw me over, said you didn't want me hangin' around. I lost my way to the stars, but look at the love I just found. You're too late, baby, too over, too, too earthbound. Can't hold this rocket, rocket, rocket."*

Now Trax and Jinx were singing with them. *"'Cause I'm a rocket, rocket, rocket . . ."* Trace looked up. Kali was standing stock-still in the doorway, probably the only person in the room who wasn't dancing. So she *had* come. And she was staring at him like he had been dipped in gold. *This*, Trace thought, *must be how it felt to be onstage . . . like everyone was in love with you.* Kali was smiling at him now, a bigger, warmer smile than he had ever expected to see from her.

*"'Cause I'm a rocket!"* the Vacationers blasted. The crescendo that Trax struck on the piano made it clear that the song was over. Celeste hugged him, made him take a bow, and then kissed him full on the lips. Trace did not have to pretend to be electrified as he stumbled into the crowd.

"*Merci, gracias, danke, bon nuit, mes chères!*"
Celeste sang into the mike, then added, "Good night and 'appy 'alloween!" Trax and Jinx had already collapsed the keyboard, and Dawoud was helping them round up the different instruments they had brought.

As Trace worked his way across the room, Presley and Ty clapped him on the back, whooping and congratulating him loudly. Auntie Lea, perched on the arm of the couch, blew him a kiss, and Dallas gave him a thumbs-up. Ahead of him, Kali was working her way straight toward him, smiling coyly. But just as she opened her mouth to say something, Angel filled the space between them and threw her arms around his neck.

"You were *ama-a-azing*!" Angel laughed, hugging him. Trace blushed. Her breath smelled of cinnamon. And just under that was the scent of fresh laundry. Trace suddenly felt he was back at the hardware store, sitting under the trees, looking up at an infinity of blue sky. Maybe this was what a flashback was. He grinned, well aware that he probably looked dopey.

"Now, this is just a good-friends thing, okay?" Angel said softly, mysteriously. He wasn't sure what she meant, but Trace nodded understandingly. And then she kissed him.

Time . . . *hiccuped*. He knew he would try to find a better way to describe this moment to himself later. But some part of his brain hit the Pause button, then restarted with a jolt. The party was winding down. Auntie Lea's playlist streamed from the speakers now, but no one seemed to be dancing anymore. At some point, the Vacationers must have left. And Kali. Kali was gone, too. He congratulated himself for not even noticing her departure. . . . *too late, baby, too over*, he thought.

Dallas had slipped on his jacket and Presley and Ty were suddenly in front of him, saying good night. Trace blinked, bringing them into focus. He watched as Angel and Roman put on their coats and Auntie Lea paced from the kitchen to the front door, doling out a doggie bag to anyone who would take one. Rico, lingering in the hallway in his overalls, with his goggles and bald cap in hand, was watching Presley's every move with wistful, hungry eyes.

Vesper and Brenda circled the room, collecting plates of chicken bones, not-quite-empty cups, crumpled napkins, half-eaten cupcakes, and used plastic forks. Trace wasn't sure where to be or what he should do. So he stood in the hallway, watching Angel tuck her wings under her coat, afraid that he might have the same look on his face that Rico did.

"Your chauffeur awaits, youse guys," Dallas said. He had borrowed Dawoud's car, and, rattling the keys, was trying to hurry Ty and Presley along. By his side, Auntie Lea stood at the door, shivering and wishing guest after guest good night. And then Angel was leaving, rolling her eyes at Rico as she dragged him away to follow Roman. But at the door, she turned, hurried down the hall, and planted another kiss on Trace's cheek.

"See you soon," was all she said. Then she was gone.

Dallas herded Ty and Presley down the stairs toward Dawoud's car, which was parked at the curb.

"Unplug the witch, will you, babe?" Auntie Lea said to him.

So Dallas was "babe" now. Trace let the word roll around his mind. Babe. Could he dare to call Angel that with a straight face? The smell of fresh laundry wafted up from his T-shirt.

As Dallas disconnected the extension cord and

the witch's glowering green face was thrown into darkness, Presley ran back up the steps and leaned around Auntie Lea.

"Oh, wow," she said loudly. "I totally blanked, Trace. This lady said to tell you thanks, and I forgot to give you the message. She was leaving when I came in. Sorry. I totally, utterly, thoroughly disremembered," she added. "Oh. And thanks, Ms. Cumberbatch, for inviting me. This was the most inimitable, superlative, stupendous party *ever*."

"What lady?" Trace asked, noticing that Presley's dictionary download had returned. At the curb, Ty was holding open the rear door of Dawoud's car. He looked cold, but he waited patiently. Dallas climbed behind the wheel and started the engine.

"Ooooh, I didn't get her name," Presley said, heading down the steps again. "She had on an old-fashioned costume, like a white pilgrim dress or something? And a black shawl?" she said over her shoulder. "A little, brown-skinned woman with braids. You know her?"

Trace shook his head, shivering as a gust of chilly air swept into the hallway. He had no idea who Presley was talking about. He was sleepy. He was cold. The only incoming message he cared about was coming from his pillow upstairs. He had some very nice things to think about when he went to sleep tonight.

"No sweat," he answered.

Presley hopped into the back seat. "Well, she seemed to know you. But it's probably one of those *things* I get," Presley called back, her breath a hazy white cloud in the darkness. Buckling herself in, she waved as Dallas pulled the car away from the curb.

# 23

The water felt good. Trace let it stream down his face as he rotated under the showerhead, wiggling his toes in the soapy puddle around his feet. Only as he toweled himself dry did it occur to him: he had not had the dream. Not last night. Not the night before. In fact, he wasn't sure when he had last dreamed that he was in the river. Very odd. Not that he missed it, but if he had done something to make it stop, it would be good to know what it was, just in case.

Scrubbing the towel through his hair, he studied his steam-blurred image in the bathroom mirror. What if the glass were to slowly clear and reveal someone else's face, staring back at him? His heart raced suddenly and Trace wiped the mirror defiantly with his towel. He knew he had been thinking of Cholly. He *had* to stop watching scary movies.

It was almost noon by the time he made it downstairs to the kitchen. Auntie Lea and Dallas sat side by side, leaning back with their elbows on the table and studying the huge board with the family tree.

"Hey, sweetie, how'd you sleep?" Auntie Lea asked, smiling over her shoulder at him. Dallas nodded warmly, one eyebrow raised, as if he knew *just* how Trace had slept.

"Good . . . um, great," Trace answered, correcting himself. He had slept *very* well. So Dallas had returned? The only surprising thing about the man still being there the morning after the party was that it felt right. Trace shook his head. Only a week ago he was convinced the guy was a psycho. Well, one of them must have changed.

His stomach growled loudly. Muffins and a bowl of diced fruit sat on the table next to a plate of . . . *bacon*? Either a meat-eating shape-shifter had possessed her or Auntie Lea must seriously like the guy.

"It's veggie bacon, Mr. Hawkeye," his aunt said pointedly. "I saw that look on your face. And no, Dallas hasn't completely converted me."

Dallas had bitten into a strip of the soy bacon and was now giving a first-rate impression of someone choking. He reached out to Trace like a drowning man. "P-p-please . . . I *know* you eat meat. Don't let the vegans get me!"

"Ha. And ha." Trace sniffed. He found yogurt in the fridge, scooped a couple of spoonfuls into a bowl, and then stirred in pieces of fruit. The plainest granola he could find was studded with goji berries—whatever those were—and he sprinkled some liberally into the mix, building his breakfast. Nina Simone's voice eased out of the speakers on the windowsill, crooning, *"Who knows where the time goes?"* as Auntie Lea hummed along.

Trace surveyed the scene. If he took a snapshot of the kitchen, they would look like an average family just having brunch and chilling. Pale sunlight filtered through the windows, bathing the whole kitchen with a lazy, Sunday afternoon softness that made the photos on the family tree almost glow. As he ate, Trace's eyes drifted across the bottom of the board and lingered on the pictures of his mom and dad. They were both smiling, both captured on sunny days under blue skies. Somewhere deep in his chest, a soft cord snagged on something, knotted itself up, and twisted slowly. But then it gently untangled and he found himself smiling back at the photos.

With Aunt Frenchy's basket at her feet, Auntie Lea leafed through old photo albums stacked on the table, setting aside an occasional picture. *"But I am not alone as long as my love is near me. And I know it will be so till it's time to go,"* she sang, slightly off-key with Nina Simone. Trace remembered the faded letter he had found.

"Check the pocket," he said. Auntie Lea turned and cocked her head. "The basket. Look in that pocket in the lining. There's a letter." His aunt grinned, bent over the basket, then sat up triumphantly, the folded yellow paper between her fingers.

"What have we here?" she said, arching her eyebrows in delight. She unfolded the paper and carefully smoothed it flat on the table. Dallas leaned over her shoulder and frowned at the letter.

"Kinda hard to read that old-timey handwriting, huh?" he said, scanning the page.

"Wow," Auntie Lea said softly, "those look like teardrop stains . . . especially at the bottom." She looked up at Trace with a sorrowful expression. "This is like looking at someone's heart break. Maybe it was to a long-lost love? Aunt Frenchy never married. So maybe Charles was the one who got away?" She looked up at Dallas, a hopeful smile at the corner of her lips.

"Wait a minute," he answered. "Right here, she writes, 'My daughters would have loved you so. Had I been blessed with a boy, he . . .' something, something, '. . . would have borne your name. But I pray yo . . . ,' another tear blotch, '. . . one day know your loving nieces, Seraphina and Sav . . .' Okay, I can't make out that part, either."

"Savannah," Trace and Auntie Lea said at the same time. They looked at each other.

"Cool. They're on the chart," Auntie Lea said, standing up. She stood in front of the board and traced her finger along the tree. "Okay, so here's great-aunt Frenchy. I *love* that picture of her," she said over her shoulder. Trace knew she wanted him to follow along, but he only nodded and turned his attention back to his breakfast. That quick look at the chart had been as much as he could handle right now. Looking too long, looking too closely, would only be pushing his luck.

"She was quite a fashionista in her day. And next

to her is my mom, Seraphina—not the one mentioned in the letter, I don't think—this Seraphina was your grandmother, kiddo. Then their little sister, Clotile. Aunt Cloudy, we called her. Theo, come check this out. I wanted to go over all this family tree stuff with you anyway." Auntie Lea turned around, hands on her hips, smiling as if they were all about to set off on an adventure.

Trace scraped the last drop of yogurt out of his bowl, then licked the spoon. His mellow mood and a guided tour of family history could not possibly co-exist. He took his bowl to the sink, rinsed it, washed it, and placed it carefully on the rack to dry.

"C'mon, Theo!" Auntie Lea said impatiently. "Look, the Seraphina in the letter must be your great-great-grandmother. Pretty cool. And her sister Savannah was, like, your great-great-aunt. She's the one your mom was named after."

Dallas was nodding and still studying the letter. "Well, whoever wrote this letter referred to them as 'your nieces,'" he said, turning to Auntie Lea. "So it wasn't Aunt Frenchy. Their mom must've written this, babe."

Trace perched on the edge of the table, one foot on

a chair, and tried to act interested. He still wanted to go over his presentation for tomorrow, because the last time he had read it through it had taken more time than he had been allotted. He didn't care if Mrs. Weaver rolled her eyes, but he didn't want Kali biting his head off. Or maybe she wouldn't? Maybe things had changed last night. But thinking about last night only made him think about Angel. Maybe he should take a walk up to Myrtle Avenue and find a reason to stop by Roman's Hardware.

"Ri-i-i-ight," Auntie Lea said, shifting her gaze up the chart. "It must have been Melissa May Ransom who wrote the letter. Boy, she looks a bit . . . grim." Auntie Lea leaned over Dallas's shoulder to study the letter, then looked up at Trace. "Check out your great-great-*great*-grandmother, Theodore."

Theodore. Auntie Lea had a definite tone in her voice now, so Trace looked up at the photo she was pointing to, ready to get this whole history moment over and done with.

"She was an orphan, so we don't know any relatives beyond her," Auntie Lea was saying. She kept talking. Going on about how cool it was to have an artifact from their oldest-known relative. Maybe she'd transcribe it, gather all these pictures up, make a book or something.

Trace heard her. But at the same time, it was as though he had gone deaf. Melissa May Ransom's photo was faded, crackled, and missing a corner. But he could see her clearly from where he sat: her tasseled black shawl glaring against a severe, white high-collared dress. A little brown-skinned woman with braids. Wait. Was she . . . ?

The doorbell jangled, nearly causing Trace to replay the "accident" he'd had at his third birthday party. He thought he heard himself gasp, but his hearing was pretty unreliable at the moment.

"I . . . I . . . I'll get it," he croaked. Auntie Lea gave him a quizzical look and then shrugged at Dallas, who just shook his head. On shaky legs, Trace headed for the door.

"So, if those were the nieces referred to in this letter," Dallas was saying, "then this Charles guy must've been her brother? He's not on the tree. You should add him, babe."

Trace threw open the door. He was ready to welcome an entire congregation of Jehovah's Witnesses if it would change the conversation. There had to be lots of little brown ladies in old-fashioned dresses on the street last night. Why was he freaking out?

"Presley!" Trace said, more relieved than surprised. "Come in, cool, great . . . good to see you!"

Presley eyed him suspiciously.

"I left my hat," she said. "And I—"

"Whatever, sure, c'mon in!" Trace nearly sang. "Where'd you leave it? Oh! You probably don't know, right? I mean that's why you left it, duh. If you'd seen it, you'd have taken it with you last night, huh? Well, I haven't seen it, but I'm sure it's around here somewhere and I'd be totally happy to look for it. But, hey. Don't just stand there! Aren'tcha freezing?"

Presley did not budge from the doorway. She was looking at him like she wasn't sure if he had finished whatever performance he was giving.

Trace tried to slow himself down. "Want cupcakes? You liked the cupcakes. You and that guy Nico, or Pico, or what was his name? Whatever. We've got tons left over. And they're still fresh, really!" He didn't want to sound desperate for company even if he was.

"Sure, okay. Yes. Coming in," Presley said evenly. She hung up her jacket on a hook in the hallway and followed Trace to the kitchen.

Trace recognized that voice. That was the voice

people used when talking to crazy people. She was using the "I'm trying to calm down an insane person" voice on *him*.

"Hi, Presley," Auntie Lea said.

"Long time, no see, Elvis," Dallas joked. Presley grinned.

"Your hat's in the front room if you're looking for it, sweetie," Auntie Lea said. "Don't suppose I could interest you in a cupcake?"

Presley beamed. "Please suppose, hypothesize, and conjecture exactly that!" Daintily lifting the cover from the tray where the cupcakes sat, Presley chose a tombstone that read, *I needed the rest!* and sat down.

"Actually, I remembered the message, Trace. From that lady who I said wanted to tell you thanks?" Presley chomped down on her cupcake, leaving a dollop of gray frosting on her upper lip that her tongue quickly swiped away.

Dallas was still bent over the letter, trying to read around the tearstains. Auntie Lea was flipping through album after album, as if on a mission. And Trace was trying to put up his shields, trying to build a force field around himself, because he knew that he did not want to hear this message. Whatever Presley had to say, whatever the woman had told her, it was going to be about that boy. He didn't know how he knew it. But he knew it.

"So, it wasn't 'thanks' exactly. She said she's *grateful*, that's the word she used. Because she couldn't go back for him, like, whoever 'him' is. She said she couldn't go back for him, but she knew *you* would . . . so she came back for you. It's like a riddle, right? Only, I don't get it. Does this make *any* sense?" Presley took another bite and turned to Auntie Lea. "These cupcakes are delicious, Ms. Cumberbatch. . . ." Her voice trailed off as she looked up at the family tree. Trace watched her head slowly lift from the photos and Post-its along the bottom to the top.

"That's her," she said flatly, turning to frown at Trace. "The lady from last night."

Dallas kept poring over the letter. Auntie Lea kept turning page after page in the photo album. But everything flipped into slow motion, giving Trace plenty of time to take stock of the situation: if that was the woman Presley saw, then Presley had seen a ghost. *Realizing* that mind-bending fact should take Presley about a nanosecond. So, any moment now, she would probably scream or burst into tears or, worst case scenario, both.

Trace watched Presley's expression ripple from alarm to confusion as she realized the woman she had seen last night had died long ago. He braced himself. Presley was about to open a door. And he felt like the whole house would collapse around it.

"Whoa," Presley breathed softly, her eyes gleaming, "she was a ghost! Cool!"

Trace had pretty much accepted that he would never understand girls. But he suspected that he would never stop trying to understand them. And knowing that was exhausting. He could only stare blankly at Presley.

She winked at him merrily and polished off her cupcake.

What was it she had been talking about that day they had taken the bus? She saw dead people? Or talked to them or listened to them or saw them floating around . . . or *something*. A normal person should be a *little* freaked out right now. But Presley was giving him some weird, hip-hoppy signals with her eyebrows, popping them up and down and jerking her head slightly toward the kitchen door.

"Well, at least this part is easy," Dallas said. He and Auntie Lea had stayed lost in the old letter and photos, somehow missing Presley's whispered word that was now clanging noisily around Trace's brain: *ghost*. Dallas held up the ancient letter.

"She's quoting from that poem 'How do I love thee? Let me count the ways' . . . it's pretty tearstained. But look, babe, she underlined the last part: *I shall but love thee better after death*. So her brother must've died."

Auntie Lea looked close to tears. "That's so sad." She peered over Dallas's shoulder and shook her head. "I think I'll add her brother, Charles, to the tree, and maybe I can find out more about him later."

"Trace," Presley said abruptly and way too politely, "will you please show me where to find my hat?" Her eyebrows had stopped twitching, but she had a crazed grin on her face that made Trace think of the smiley-face emoticon.

"S . . . s . . . sure, Presley," he said, pushing back his chair.

Auntie Lea looked up from the index card she was

writing out. "The hat's in the front room, guys," she said distractedly. And to Dallas she said, "So 'Charles' is all it says, right? No other details?"

"Mmmm-hmmm," Dallas said.

Trace and Presley had reached the kitchen door.

"Wait a minute!" Dallas said. "Here she writes, 'Forgive me, my dear, sweet Cholly.'" The man's head swiveled sharply toward Trace and their eyes locked.

Trace froze. Presley froze too.

"'Kay, thanks. Probably only a nickname, but you never know, it might help." Auntie Lea bent over the card to write *Cholly* in parentheses. Dallas crooked his head slightly and frowned questioningly at Trace.

"My hat," Presley insisted. She grabbed Trace's hand and pulled him toward the front room before he could do more than shrug at Dallas.

"Look," Presley said once they were alone. "Don't ask me how I know, but I *know* that I know, okay? I'm just not sure *what* I know I know, you know?"

Presley trained her eyes steadily on his and Trace could only nod. For some reason, that made sense. She was weird. Scary weird. But he knew she was trying to help him.

"That lady I saw? I'm pretty sure it was your

great-great-great dead whatever, okay? And the *him* she was talking about? I'm pretty sure she was talking about that Cholly guy she was writing to in her letter. That name just clicked for me suddenly."

Presley was waiting for a response, but Trace just sat down on the couch and shook his head slightly. Pieces of a puzzle seemed to be scattered all around him . . . not that there were so many, really, but he had no idea how they all fit together.

"I don't like to brag, but this kinda stuff is my gift," Presley said proudly. "My forte, my specialty, my strong suit, my—"

"I get it," Trace said, looking up at her. She seemed to almost glow in the cool gray light of the unlit room. He believed her. What surprised him even more was that he trusted her. "Do you know anything about what happened to me?" he asked quietly.

Presley picked up her Abe Lincoln hat, sat down on the couch next to him, and rested it solemnly on her lap. "Tell me," she said.

And so he did. Trace went back to the highway and the flash of a deer leaping from the woods, took himself willingly into the back seat of the car and to its slow, desperate plunge into the river. He told Presley about the water rising, about his dad kicking and about the way his mom had turned toward him, twisting around in her seat, searching his eyes. He had to stop for a minute. He tucked his head in his lap, trying to shake off the dizziness that came with the memory of his mom's face. He didn't worry about what Presley might think; he simply took deep breaths until his head cleared.

"The windows were closed, Presley," he said finally, sitting up straight and looking into her eyes. "I have a newspaper clipping that shows the car after they pulled it out of the river. They were closed. So how did I get out? I know that someone pulled me out, I saw her hands, I felt them. I can still feel them sometimes. But how? When it was happening, I never thought *how*? I wasn't thinking anything—except maybe *Help!* or *Air!* or *I don't want to die!* you know?" Trace met Presley's eyes. "A pair of long, brown, *bare* arms came for me. Grabbed me and pulled me right through the window. The window Dad couldn't break. And when I hit the surface, these two EMT guys lifted me onto a raft or something. Two guys in *uniforms*." Trace shook his head.

"Okay. Strange. Definitely. Gotta think about that.

But tell me about this Cholly," Presley said.

Suddenly, Dallas was standing in the doorway, a concerned look on his face. "I have to run to my workshop for bit," he said. "You guys want to come?"

Dallas drove.

"I think we need to regroup," he had said after pulling the car out into traffic. "I haven't said anything to your Auntie Lea, and I think I get why you'd rather not tell her. At least not yet. But what are the odds of that name, Theo? If you're related to this Cholly, you're going to need to let her in on this." He added in a quieter voice, "I'm guessing you've told Presley about *things*?"

Trace only nodded at Dallas. Sitting in the front seat, he watched Presley through the side-view mirror, where she was belted into the back seat and staring silently out the window.

"So, Presley, that day I was supposed to meet you guys in the library, remember?" he asked over his shoulder. "Something happened." And then he told her *almost* everything—about the stacks, about the boy in tatters, and about the guards. He left out his opinion of Lemuel T. Spitz. There was a chance, although

Trace thought it a slim one, that Dallas was actually friends with the guy. But he did tell her about the smoke and his suspicion that it was connected to the draft riots fire. Finally, he told Presley about the toy rattle, only leaving out the fact that it had disappeared when Cholly did. He hadn't told Dallas that bit either, and he wasn't sure why.

"So that's why it burned my hand," Presley said as though talking to herself.

They were inching onto the Brooklyn Bridge, and Trace studied the twin stone arches towering before them. Normally, they made him think of castle walls, of fortresses and moats. But today they were making his head swim. Everything—this bridge, the trees in City Hall Park, the traffic lights, every building they were passing—had been left behind by people who were long dead. How did that make any sense? People died, but the things they made survived. For ages. How could that rattle have held on to the heat of the fire? If his iPod had ended up in the river and someone ever fished it out, if it washed up on the bank and was found by someone like Presley, someone who heard things, saw things, felt things . . . what kind of sounds would it make? Trace leaned his head against the cool glass of the window. Sometimes he missed his parents so badly that his skin burned.

"This time last year, I was in New Orleans," Presley said, breaking into his thoughts, her voice raised to combat the sounds of the traffic around them. They were zooming up Sixth Avenue at a nice clip now; the Sunday afternoon traffic was very light. "My Granny Taylor lives there in a big old house that used to give me the heebie-jeebies. Yeccccchhhh! Creepy with a capital *K*! And *pleeeeeeease* don't ask me for details!" No one did.

Dallas smiled at her in the rearview mirror. Trace merely waited.

"Trace, you know about All Souls Day, Day of the Dead and all that?" She didn't wait for an answer. "In Mexico it's called *El Día de los Muertos*." Presley leaned forward and lowered her voice dramatically. "The gates of heaven open at the crack of midnight on Halloween to let all the spirits of the dead come back to visit their families for, like, a whole day. There's like a window, an aperture, a perforation . . . a *peephole* in the universe. And, let me tell you, they take this *realllllll* seriously in Looooosiana! Granny Taylor made us troop around to family graves—well, to family gravestones, anyway. They had a big flood down there long ago, right? So no one knows who's buried where anymore, which is crazy. Coffins just popped up outa the mud in the graveyards and started floating around. When the water finally receded, they stuck 'em back in the ground every which way. Can you imagine?"

Trace couldn't imagine. He didn't want to imagine. Dallas threw him a quizzical, sideways glance but said nothing. They turned onto West Fortieth Street and Dallas slowed down to look for a parking space.

"Anyway, Granny Taylor says this is the absolutely best, consummately, unequaled, hands-down el primo time of the year for a palaver with the dead."

Dallas grinned at her in the rearview mirror. "Let's just see if we can think through this thing, okay?" He edged the car into a parking space near the corner of Fifth Avenue.

They were out of the car, around the corner, and climbing the stairs between the lions minutes later. Once they were in the elevator, Dallas turned his key in the control panel that would let them into the stacks.

"I told your aunt I could scan the letter and maybe

show it to someone," Dallas explained. "There are folks working here who are experts at reading old documents." Before Trace could say anything, the elevator doors dinged open and the three of them were greeted by the smell of cold, damp earth.

"Whoa," said Presley. The stacks yawned before them.

**25**

The wavering wall of wilted fortune slips was a big hit with Presley.

"Brilliant idea, Mr. Houston," was how she had put it after slipping off her coat.

The minute they arrived, Dallas had made a quick phone call, then brewed a pot of hot chocolate. He was idly leafing through papers on his worktable as Presley examined every nook and cranny in the workshop. "So . . . what I was thinking," Dallas began, "was that I could get someone down here to read the letter and maybe we can figure out enough to make some educated guesses about the rest." He paused. "Okay? First of all, what do we actually know?" Dallas and

Presley both looked at Trace expectantly.

But Trace was staring at the corner where he had last seen Cholly. There was no toy on the floor, no electrical buzz in the air, not the slightest whiff of smoke, *nada*. Had it all been his imagination on overload? Dallas and Presley were waiting, but a serious discussion about ghosts, whether it was All Souls or All Saints or *El Día de los Zombies*, suddenly seemed ridiculous.

"So, you saw this kid, right? And he said his name was Cholly?" Dallas prompted.

"Um, yeah, sure," Trace agreed. "He was waiting for his sister, I think." Trace tried to recall the boy's exact words. "Sissy. He called her Sissy. I thought he was calling me names." Trace chuckled, trying to lighten the mood. But just saying those names aloud had given weight to his memories.

"Well, your great-great-great grandmother's name *was* Melissa, so Sissy could easily have been what her little brother would have called her," Dallas said. "Did you notice her dates on your Auntie Lea's family tree? She was born in 1856. So by the time of the draft riots she would've been, what?"

"The riots started on July 13, 1863," Trace said quickly, glad to have something as concrete as math to think about. "So she would've been around seven years old at the time of the fire."

Dallas smoothed the letter out on the tabletop just as someone knocked loudly on the door. Both Trace and Presley jumped.

"You rang, Tex?" The woman from the front desk with the cotton-candy hair was leaning in the doorway.

"C'mon in, Margaret. Meet my friends. This is Theo and his friend Presley. We're tryin' to do some historical research and I just knew you were the one who could help us." Dallas got up from the stool he had been occupying, the most comfortable one in the room, and offered it to the woman.

Presley rolled her eyes at Trace. He knew he was going to hear about Margaret later. The woman wore a jumble of colors that seemed to bounce against one another as she waltzed over to accept the stool. Her hair now had a purple tinge to it.

"Hello, *children*," she drawled in a curious accent. Her heavily dusted green eyelids half closed as she eyed them. "Now, what sort of research might I help with?" she asked Dallas.

Before he could answer, the woman was leaning over the opened letter, drawing a long, lavender nail across the writing. Blinking rapidly, she set small green clouds of powder adrift as she read.

"Mid-nineteenth century, American, definitely not an upper-class hand," she announced confidently. Dallas nodded, then winked at Trace, as though Margaret's expertise had just been confirmed.

"We were hoping you'd have an easier time reading this than we've had, Margaret," he said. "It's a family letter, but you see there's no date. And some damaged areas too that—"

"Tears," Margaret stated firmly. "Yes, I see. This is written in a woman's hand. Ahh, yes," she continued, her eyes dropping to the bottom of the page, "*M-e*-blank-*iss*—probably it is from a *Melissa*?" She shrugged at her guess. "*Verrrrrry* popular name at the time," she added, rolling her *r*'s dramatically.

And then she began to read from the top, slowly, in her weird drawl, as Dallas hovered discreetly by her shoulder. "*Dearest Charles . . .*'" Trace felt a slight shift in the air; a barely noticeable current of electricity seemed to run through him. Looking up, he saw that Presley was staring at the same corner where he had seen Cholly. It took every ounce of his will to follow her gaze, worried about what he might—or might *not*—see.

"'*I was pulled away, crying for them to let me save . . .*' Ahhh, these water marks are everywhere. I see why you've had such difficulty. '. . . *def to my words, so furrus was the heat and smoke.*" Margaret paused to point out to Dallas the line she had just read. "See here, how she misspells *furious* and *deaf*? I think whoever wrote was quite distraught and hurrying to get her thoughts down, Mr. Texas." She gave Dallas a forlorn smile, her lips disappearing into a thin, red line.

Trace was watching the corner of the room. Something was changing. In the same way that he had seen air quiver over hot asphalt on a summer day, the area where Cholly had crouched had begun to shimmer slightly. Was Presley seeing this? He turned to look, but she was sipping her hot chocolate and watching Margaret intently, a frown of concentration on her face.

Trace heard the scrabbled, piecemeal words as Margaret read them aloud, absorbing their emotion, surprised that complete, logical sentences did not seem necessary. He understood. He got it. Melissa was sorry. She had lived her whole life being sorry. She had tried to save her brother, but "they" did not believe a child had been left behind. "They" were in charge. And "they" had dragged her to safety. A safety she had regretted and cried over and resented for what it had cost her until the day she died.

"*I could not come back for you*," Margaret read, "*but you are always with me*." She let out a long sigh.

"She is writing to the dead, you know. And this poem, one of Elizabeth Barrett Browning's sonnets—you're familiar with it, I'm sure, Tex?" Margaret said to Dallas. "'How Do I Love Thee?' Browning published it in the 1850s, I believe. So at least we know that this letter was written around that time or after it." Margaret held up the letter, lowered her green eyelids, and read dramatically, "'I love thee with the breath / Smiles, tears, of all my life; and, if God choose, / I shall but love thee better after death.'"

The corner seemed alive now. The two bare walls

that met looked just as wavery to Trace as the one with the Chinese fortunes. He blinked. And there was Cholly.

"*Forgive me, my dear, sweet Cholly,*" Margaret read in her peculiar accent, her voice sounding far away and sad, as though the words were draining her. Trace listened. He saw that Cholly was listening too, aware that every word, every tearstain had been just for him. The boy's face was soft-edged and bathed in some light that Trace realized was not in the room.

"You can have the paper analyzed to get a better sense of its age," Margaret was saying to Dallas. Trace heard the letter rustle softly, knew that she was turning it over in her long, thin hands. But he kept his eyes on Cholly. Cholly, the lost little boy with the big wet eyes who must have been alone and terrified when an angry mob burned down his home. Cholly, or maybe just a memory of Cholly that was trapped here, like an image on film, in these dark halls, waiting for a sister who could not come. Cholly, who, if any of this was real, was his own great-great-great-great-uncle.

Trace wanted to cry; he wanted to hug the little boy and tell him that he was sorry. Sorry that Sissy couldn't save him. He wanted to read those words to

Cholly himself, tell him that his sister never meant to leave him; she loved him and even death would never change that. But he only smiled.

And Cholly smiled back.

Message delivered.

"That won't be necessary, Margaret," Dallas said behind him. "Thanks, though. This was helpful, right, guys?"

His voice seemed to break a circuit, turning off the electricity in the room. Trace glanced quickly at Presley. She looked as though she had just awakened. "Yes, th . . . thanks. Thank you," he said politely, nodding as Margaret stood to leave.

"Be right back, guys," Dallas said, walking Margaret out the door.

"Was Cholly here?" Presley asked quietly. She had gotten up from the couch where she'd been sitting and walked straight over to the corner. Stooping down, she picked up the metal rattle, stood, and ran her fingers over it.

It was back! Trace shook his head slowly. Cholly was really gone.

"It doesn't burn," she said, holding it out to Trace. "The heat is gone."

Trace took the rattle, turned it over in his hands, then slipped it into his jacket pocket. It hadn't been there when they came in. He was certain of that. "Did you . . . could you see him?" he asked.

Presley shook her head. "I felt somebody here, in that corner, to be exact. But no, I didn't see Cholly. He was here for you."

Dallas bustled back into the room, rubbing his hands together excitedly. "So you may be right, Theo! That letter does make it sound like this Melissa and her younger brother got caught up in the fire. And, if this really was your great-great whatever, then it sorta makes sense that you're the one who can see him, right?"

Trace just nodded. He felt sure that Cholly was gone. This was finished. Wherever Cholly was, he could rest now.

"What do you say we let your Auntie Lea in on this story? She might even get into it, do a bit more research, you know?" Dallas continued as he rinsed out the mugs they had used. He reached for his jacket and Presley slipped into her coat.

"Sure," Trace said. It really was over.

Dallas held the door and Trace followed Presley out

into the stacks. It was just a gloomy, dusky space now, without a lick of electricity in the air.

"Margaret's a colorful character, but she was enlightening, right?" Dallas asked as they headed for the elevator.

"Prismatic, vibrant, even kaleidoscopic," Presley agreed.

Trace just nodded again and gave Dallas a weak smile.

Lying in the darkness of his room later that night, Trace studied the rectangle of faint light that was his window. That window, he could almost hear Mrs. Madden say, is a metaphor. There was light beyond the darkness of his room, light beyond Cholly's long wait. For the first time, he felt there might be light beyond the hard, guilty ache that had rooted in his chest. Suddenly, he needed to see his parents' pictures again.

Trace slid out of the covers and climbed down from his loft bed. The floor was cold on his bare feet, but he left his shoes off, not wanting to wake Auntie Lea. He left the lights off too and tiptoed downstairs to the kitchen, one hand on the banister, one on the wall to steady himself. The same moonlight from the backyard was throwing skewed squares of spotlight across the kitchen wall that held the family tree. In the dark kitchen, the two faces he loved were lit up, bathed in a soft blue glow that he knew would forever be the sunlight in which the camera had captured them. Trace ran his thumb along the outline of their smiles. It was all good.

# 26

"So, we've got this, right, team?" Ty said confidently. Presley gave him a thumbs-up sign, Kali sighed heavily, and Trace simply nodded. With three minutes left before class started, the noise level in the room had reached critical mass. Conversations buzzed, chairs scraped, and laughter erupted around them as books, bags, and butts thumped onto desks and into seats.

"Good afternoon, class," Mrs. Weaver said crisply, scanning everyone over the top of her eyeglasses as she closed the door behind her. "I trust you ramstuginous boodle of would-be scholars are prepared to finish up the 1800s today?"

"*Whaaaaaa'd* she just call us?" Yolanda Stringer

huffed, sliding into her seat next to Dani Perez.

"Anyone attempting to absquatulate before we are done or to hornswoggle me with excuses today will be exfluncticated," the teacher continued. All eyes were on her now, the silence in the room complete. Even the old wall clock muffled the soft clunking of its second hand.

Suddenly, Lou Pagano burst through the door. "Yo, yo, yo, Mrs. W., I know it *looks* like I'm late, but trust me, I got mad explanations! Wha' happened wuz . . ." He trailed off, freezing as he surveyed the silent room. "S'up wit you guys?"

Mrs. Weaver pushed up the sleeves of her sweater, contemplated him coolly, and said, "Take your seat, Mr. Pagano. And pull up those inexpressibles!"

Lou's face contorted in confusion. Hurrying to his seat, he yanked his pants up and sat down behind Presley, who was grinning merrily.

"Now *what* did I just say, class?" Mrs. Weaver asked, a hint of mischief in her eyes. Presley's arm shot up, nearly out of its socket. She fluttered her hand wildly at the teacher.

"Yes, Presley?"

"Slang. Not sure what all of it was, but that's

old-fashioned slang, right?" Presley said proudly.

"Precisely." Mrs. Weaver turned toward the board and listed her curious words next to their brief explanations:

*ramstuginous*—rambunctious, rowdy

*boodles*—crowds

*absquatulate*—to leave

*hornswoggle*—to mislead or trick

*exfluncticated*—completely destroyed

"And in the 1800s," she continued, "you might be surprised that *inexpressibles* was considered a vulgar word. Its meaning, Mr. Pagano?" The teacher turned her gaze on a distraught-looking Lou.

"Um, my pants?" he guessed sheepishly.

"Pants!" Mrs. Weaver cried sharply. Yolanda Stringer jumped in her seat.

"History didn't just happen a long time ago," the teacher continued. "It's happening now. You're making it. Think about it. You are doing reports on the memorable things people did in the 1800s. But they didn't think of themselves as being 'history.' They were people like your mom and dad, your best friend, the guy in the corner store. They knew the latest dances, they wore the coolest fashions, and they used slang words that drove their parents mad. They just did it a hundred or so years before you got here. And in another hundred years, guess what? Someone might be sitting right where you're sitting, writing a report about *you*."

Lou's mouth was open, his face a mask of disbelief.

Mrs. Weaver brushed the chalk off her hands, pushed her glasses up her nose, and turned to Trace. "Mr. Carter, Ms. Presley, Mr. Lee, Ms. Castleberry: Are the 1860s ready to go?"

From the front of the room where they had lined up, Trace could read the mood of the class in a glance: they weren't expecting much. Another list of facts, another fifteen minutes of another group droning on about another decade. But this was *his* group. They hadn't divvied up topics or worried about chronological order. They had chosen whatever appealed to them. Well, at least, the others had. He had taken what he had assumed would be the boring leftovers. Grinning at that thought, Trace looked down the line to see if his team was ready. Kali, at the other end, grinned back. At him. Wild. And then she stepped forward, going first, because, well, she was Kali.

"How much would you pay to mail a birthday card?"

she asked the class. "In 1860 it cost five dollars just to send a letter. That would've been one hundred and thirty-five bucks in today's money. Pony Express riders earned twenty-five dollars a week, which was big time compared to the dollar a week that regular jobs paid. So, still want to send that birthday card? Well, five weeks of work and you got it covered." There were a few grunts of disbelief.

Speeding through the *who, why, what*, and *how* of the Pony Express, Kali deftly arrived at the *where*: "The headquarters in Saint Joseph, Missouri, was just blocks from where Jesse James was killed, shot in the back of the head by one of his *pardners* while he was hanging up a picture." Kali unreeled the infamous outlaw's story, bringing to life a minister's son gone bad, or maybe *turned* bad by misfortune and abuse at the hands of Union soldiers. She read from a letter he'd written to a little girl's family, offering to pay her medical expenses after he'd accidentally shot her while making a getaway.

When Trace had been trying to impress Kali, he had learned that a Kansas City newsman had helped Jesse James shape his image into that of a folk hero.

So a thieving, murderous, publicity-hungry gangster could rob banks, hold up trains, shoot soldiers *and* little girls and still be a rock star. His. Story. Trace nearly laughed out loud: it had always been right there in the word. History. Apparently, everything depended on who was telling the tale.

"And, finally," Kali said, "Black Friday. That was the day the whole stock market crashed because two shady bankers had been hoarding gold." She whipped a gold bar out of her purse. From where Trace stood, it looked like the real thing. Impressive show-and-tell, he thought, but that gold bar could've been bought yesterday. Still, like his dad always said, "Great minds think alike." Trace wrapped his fingers protectively around the tin rattle in his pocket. His was the real deal.

"Gold," Kali purred, holding the bar to her cheek and nuzzling it as though she were in love with it. Everyone, even Trace, seemed to lean toward her, hypnotized by the golden glow lighting her face. Suddenly, she turned and stared icily at the class. "On September 24, 1869, the military had to be called out because people were hanging bankers from lampposts in the street—all because of greed"—Kali lowered her voice dramatically as she handed the gold bar to Damon to pass around the class—"for *this*!"

Damon pretended to try to bite into the bar. But Kali merely narrowed her eyes in his direction and he quickly passed it on to Haeyoun behind him. Everyone's eyes followed the gold bar, waiting for it to come their way, to turn it over and wonder if it was real. Trace was glad he was not up next, because no one was watching the front of the room anymore.

Tiberius calmly stepped forward and aimed a remote at the projector sitting atop the vents lining the windows. Presley went quickly to the door and turned off the lights. Trace hadn't noticed that the wall opposite the projector had been cleared of posters and charts until it lit up with Ty's presentation. A map of the United States as it appeared in 1860 glowed on the wall. As Ty narrated, the state of South Carolina peeled away, followed by Mississippi, Florida, Alabama, and Georgia. It was pretty impressive, the colorful state shapes lifting off the map in the order they had left the Union, curling one by one off the edge of the screen. Then the state of Kansas floated in and plastered itself into position as Texas began to peel.

"There were battles," Ty said ominously. He reeled off a list of names Trace recognized, like Fort Sumter and Gettysburg, and so many more that he had never heard before. Images of Confederate and Yankee soldiers, clips from documentaries and films that must have taken days for Ty to assemble, played across the wall to the soft strains of the "Battle Hymn of the Republic."

"The Battle of Antietam, in Maryland, was the bloodiest single day in American history, with 23,000 men killed, missing, or wounded," Ty said. On the screen, soldiers moved in a slow-motion battle as Ty quoted descriptions of the war from actual letters: *shells whizzed overhead, limbs were blown away, men shrieked in pain.* As the video faded, Ty read, "'*I came upon a lifeless form . . . a boy of just seventeen years, no more . . . his lips, his eyes, sewn freshly closed by death.*' Antietam, September 17, 1862." There was a hush in the room. Seventeen seemed too real.

Ty looked up from his notes, then went and flipped the lights back on as Presley stepped forward. Holding a stack of poster boards nearly as tall as herself, she pivoted from side to side, showing off the top board: a blown-up, sepia-toned photo of a child sitting in a lopsided and lumpy armchair. "Okay," she said. "The *idea* of the camera has been around since a scientist in Iraq described one, way back in 1029. The earliest surviving photograph was taken in the 1820s, but it took till the 1860s to take pictures with a shorter exposure time. No big deal, you say? Well, it *used ta* take hours to get an image on film. And children were, like, the *most* horrible, problematic, totally vexatious subjects." Presley grinned slyly at the class. "Now, this *looks* like a kid in a chair, right?"

Foreheads furrowed in the front row as students leaned forward to study the photo. Eyebrows arched and shoulders shrugged in the back rows. Mrs. Weaver's head cocked to one side.

"But that's no chair, you guys. That's the kid's mom—in a chair costume! Totally insane, right? But until 1866, that was one way they got kids to sit still long enough to get the shot." An appreciative chorus of *Whoa!*s and *No way!*s rippled through the class.

Grinning broadly, Presley quickly rattled off random facts about the first US income tax and the stock exchange opening in New York. She breezed through the invention of dynamite, paused at the purchase of Alaska, "for, like, two cents an acre, you guys!" and then held up a collage of Wyoming, a ballot box, and a little old lady. A banner reading *Grandma Swain, 1st to cast her ballot after Wyoming gave women the vote* was painted across the top.

Trace checked the clock. Presley was flying through dates and events, but she had less than two minutes left.

"Abraham Lincoln was the first president with a beard," she said, holding up an image of an old letter that was impossible to read. "This is a letter from one eleven-year-old Grace Bedell. She wrote to tell him that 'All the ladies like whiskers' and that she would try to get people to vote for him if he would only grow a beard. And so . . . he did! A mondo beyondo hair fact, but totally true!"

Mrs. Weaver screwed up her mouth but said nothing.

Presley pulled out another board, turning left and right so the whole class could see it. "His famous stove-pipe hat was often stuffed with important documents, and his cat ate dinner with him at the dining room table." The painting she held looked like it was still wet. It showed the president, Mrs. Lincoln, and a large, wild-eyed cat sitting before plates of fried chicken, corn on the cob, and some kind of leafy green clumps. At Abe's elbow was his hat, upturned and stuffed with papers. But it was a massive cake, in the center of the table, that had gotten most of Presley's artistic attention. Trace recognized the red, white, and blue frosted bunting that laced the pink cake. It was the Fourth of July signature dessert at Carvel last summer.

"Abraham Lincoln was the first president to be assassinated," Presley concluded, briefly describing the politics that led to his unfortunate evening at the theater. Her last board showed a photograph taken at Lincoln's inauguration. Standing in the background behind the president, in grainy black and white, was his future assassin, John Wilkes Booth. That got enough oohs and aahs to egg her on.

"If we have time for Q and A," she added merrily, "ask me about Lincoln's ghost, okay? He's not just in the Lincoln bedroom! He pops up all over the White House, freaks out the staff—"

"Thank you, Presley, let's save that for later," Mrs. Weaver interjected firmly. "Mr. Carter, would you kindly finish up the sixties?"

Trace cleared his throat. Of course Presley would end with ghosts. All eyes turned toward him now.

"It's 1861," Trace began. "You're six years old. The Civil War breaks out, but you don't have a clue what that means. You're a slave. You work from the time the sun comes up till the time it goes down. Feeding chickens. Carrying water. Your little hands are blistered. Your feet ache. And you're always, *always* hungry.

"And then you're eight. It's 1863. *President Lincoln has issued the Emancipation Proclamation*, someone whispers. What does that *mean*? You're free, they say. But you're not. Your parents are dead. Or sold. Or just gone. You and your little brother are in an orphanage. At least you're together, you think."

Trace looked up. A little bit of everything looked back at him: white, black, Hispanic, Asian, and more. Suddenly, he could believe that they really were caught up in a river of time. Their ancestors really had fought one another, bought, sold, and served one another, even married one another. And now here they all sat, crazily mixed together. He glanced at his notes.

Reading mechanically, he talked about the promise of Reconstruction and the Homestead Act that helped freed slaves secure land. He described the Ku Klux Klan, masked white men who terrorized black people, destroying their property and lynching them to suppress any hope they had of ever living freely. "Things may change," he said, "but the KKK still exists. There are fewer members now, but they haven't changed."

The distinct feeling of being in a river washed over him and Trace took a deep breath. This river felt different though. It felt right. It was as if he could see himself flowing along in a stream of time. And he wasn't alone. They were all in it. All the faces in front of him, all the people he had met since coming to Brooklyn, his whole family . . . they were all moving along with him, moving through time. Soft clunks from the clock brought him back to his report.

"The draft riots began July 13, 1863. White men who couldn't afford to buy their way out of it were drafted to fight in the Civil War. Many were angry, and gangs turned into crowds. The crowds gathered steam, looking for black people to lynch. They rioted, assaulted police, burned down property. Then they set fire to the Colored Orphan Asylum. And you're eight. You live there. You hear the yelling, smell the smoke, you're terrified because you know that they're coming for *you*. So you run. Nurses grab your hand and you let yourself be pulled along. You run for your life. But your little brother?"

Trace had kept his hand in his pocket, closed tightly around the rattle. He saw the worry on everyone's faces. Ty and Presley, and even Kali, looked distressed. They were all there with him in the orphanage. All hoping the little brother would be reached in time. Trace took a deep breath. In time. Cholly really had waited.

His voice cracked a little. "You know your brother will stay put. Down there in a dark room, even with smoke filling the air, he will wait for you. So you try to go back, try to convince the adults that your baby brother is *not* one of the running children, *not* with other nurses, *not* safely through that rear door. You know he's not, because the last thing you told him was to wait. You said you'd be back. With this." Trace pulled the rattle out of his pocket and laid it on the palm of his hand.

"Good heavens," Mrs. Weaver gasped. "Do you know if that's real?"

Trace turned toward the teacher. "What I know is that this is a tin toy from the time of the Civil War. I know that my great-great-great-grandmother kept it, and that it had belonged to her younger brother. What I believe is that they were caught up in the draft riots and that she survived but he did not. What I *know* is that we are all part of history just like you said, Mrs. Weaver. And I know that this toy belonged to a little kid who may not have shown up in any records, but he was my great-great-great uncle, Charles Ransom."

For a moment, no one said a word. Then Lou Pagano began clapping. To Trace's surprise, the whole class broke out in applause. Ty nudged him. Presley gave him a thumbs-up. He might have imagined it, but he thought Kali winked. Even the Elvis vase on the teacher's desk seemed to be grinning.

"History is a lively place indeed!" Mrs. Weaver beamed. "Well, done, 1860s. Well done!" The teacher blinked and readjusted her glasses. "Now, *hopefully* the 1870s were equally as eventful?" An uncomfortable silence followed.

Yolanda Stringer gulped. Dani and Damon carried a diorama of what looked like a stable to the front of the room. A sign taped above it read *Mrs. O'Leary's cowshed, Chicago 1871.* Taking a large plastic cow from her book bag, Yolanda joined them at the front of the room, set it down on the straw that covered the bottom of the diorama, pulled a stack of index cards from her jeans pocket, and turned glumly to face the class. She looked at everyone like she wished she had matches.

# 27

"Whaddya think, sunspots? Lithium in the water supply? Some kinda alien brain invasion?" Ty was shaking his head in wonder.

"Hey, we rocked that report," Presley said. "That's why."

Kali had just treated the three of them to smoothies at the café on Bergen Street. *And* hung out with them, clearly enjoying the buzz they all felt after their presentation. With eyes and voice dramatically lowered, she had even shared her tragic life story: growing up with an ex-model mom, a mysterious and wealthy dad, too many nannies, managers, and maids, constantly jetting around the planet. Trace kept a straight face.

Didn't fabulously wealthy daughters of superstars go to private schools? Or travel with tutors? Just mixing with the mere mortals at IS 99 had to be difficult, so he didn't ask her *why* she did.

By the time they headed for the train, the sky was streaked with hot pinks and oranges. "Maybe she's always been a secretly nice person," Presley said, watching Kali hop into a town car that had magically appeared.

"And maybe Lou Pagano is really Einstein's long-lost grandson." Ty laughed, shaking his head.

Trace nodded. "Hey, keep hope alive."

The G train was packed, with only one seat unoccupied as they boarded. With ninja-like precision, Presley whipped off her backpack and sent it whizzing across the aisle. The woman sitting next to where it landed only raised an eyebrow as it thunked into the spot, ruffling her newspaper. A smattering of applause broke out in the car as Presley claimed the seat.

Trace and Ty worked their way over to where she sat and leaned over her, impressed with her skills. Trace only caught bits of the choppy conversation Ty and Presley were having . . . *real gold bar?* . . .

*banana smoothie? . . . when did she text for her car?*
He watched their reflections in the darkened window
before him: they looked just like any other cluster
of kids he saw on the subway after school. Like any
group of friends.

Ty lived two stops beyond theirs, so Trace found
himself walking home alone with Presley. When the
two of them finally emerged onto Washington Avenue, the sky was a deep twilight blue. All along the
street, glowing windows offered peeks at book-lined
walls, cozy kitchens, and curtained dining rooms. He
listened as Presley downloaded every drop of fact, fantasy, and gossip she had.

"Twin NASA scientists live over there," she said,
lowering her voice and jerking her head toward a prim
brick building across the street. In the window, Trace
saw a grand piano surrounded by leafy plants. "One
was locked in an isolation tank for a year, went *completely* insane. Bonkers, psychotic, deranged. Do *not*
stop if one of them comes out, okay? No way you'll
know which one you're getting.

"Hey, this is me," she said, stopping suddenly in
front of one of the few carriage houses on the block.

Trace had passed it many times, always amused by the colorful collection of painted animals that lined an upstairs window.

"I . . . um, you want to come in?" Presley asked.

"Another time," Trace said, surprised to realize that he meant it. "Those animals are really cool," he added. Presley beamed.

"'Kay. See you tomorrow." Presley dug into a pocket in her jacket, retrieved an overloaded key chain, and deftly singled out one key. Trace waited politely as she opened her door.

"We *did* rock the sixties," she said, grinning.

Trace nodded. "Tomorrow, kiddo," he said.

Trace turned onto Myrtle Avenue. Up ahead he could see the awning over Roman's Hardware store, still outlined by a string of orange Halloween lights. The street was crawling with taxis, all headed back to Manhattan after safely dropping off their passengers. He pulled his jacket collar higher, wishing he hadn't left his wool scarf at home that morning.

Home.

Trace hurried up the steps to 810 Vanderbilt and slid his key into the lock. Shrugging off his jacket, he inhaled the buttery scent emanating from the kitchen. Potatoes. No idea what would be with them, but potatoes were definitely on the menu. He reached the kitchen door just as strains of airy flute music unfurled from the speakers.

Auntie Lea looked up at him from the table where she was arranging ingredients for a mammoth salad. "'El Condor Pasa,' señor," she said, smiling. "Do you know that there are over thirty-five hundred different kinds of potatoes in Peru? Thirty-five *hundred*!"

"And we're having . . . ?" Trace asked.

"Hah! Don't you worry, mister. Just come help me with this salad if you don't have too much homework, okay?" Auntie Lea got up, peered in the oven, and then checked a pot that was boiling on the stove.

"Gimme three minutes," Trace replied.

He took the stairs two at a time, parked his book bag, kicked off his shoes, and grabbed his comfy sweatshirt from the closet. He was starving. Above him, on the closet shelf, a corner of the box he had been avoiding hung provocatively over the edge. Trace pulled it down, spilling several photos to the floor in the process. There they were. Mom. Dad. Him.

Scooping up the pictures, Trace sat down at his desk with the box. He pulled out one that his mom had taken of him only last spring, her thumb blotting out a corner. Knowing Auntie Lea would get a kick out of her sister's photography skills, he tucked the picture into his pocket. There were so many photos. And he was ready to look at them. He *needed* to look at them. It was time to put them on the wall where he could see them every day, where they could see him. Just then, the doorbell rang.

Ahh. Cuties were in the house. He'd better get the salad going. Trace slid the box to the side. They would be there.

When he got downstairs, there was only Dallas in the kitchen, sleeves rolled up, slicing cheese into a blender.

"Trace, my man! Just in time to watch your perfectly pretty aunt peel pounds of purple Peruvian potatoes." Dallas laughed at his own tongue twister. "Grab an onion for me, will ya? We're having papa a la Huancaína."

Trace only raised an eyebrow.

"*Wan-kay-eena*. You'll love it, trust me. It's *very*

cheesy." Dallas began whistling as another flute song filled the air.

Trace quickly washed his hands, pulled an onion from the fridge, a *vowel vegetable*, he noted, and tossed it to Dallas. Then he started chopping carrots and celery and tearing apart a head of lettuce. While everything was bubbling, baking, simmering, and sizzling, Trace pulled the photo out of his pocket. He studied the family tree chart for a minute, then pulled off the Post-it note stuck at the bottom that read *Theodore Raymond Carter*. He looked around for a piece of tape.

"Use this," Auntie Lea said, holding out a pushpin. She was standing right behind him, smiling. Trace stuck his photo on the board, and as he stepped back to admire it, his aunt wrapped an arm around his shoulders. There they all were. In photos and clippings, sometimes with notes scrawled on torn scraps of paper, there was his family, from Melissa and Cholly down to Mom, Dad, him, and Auntie Lea.

He would tell her tonight about Cholly. And about the arms that had pulled him free of the car. Trace shook his head. Auntie Lea was going to love this: rescued by one ghost to go save another. Maybe later, when he could get into his thinking position, he would figure out why on earth this all felt so right.

Auntie Lea gave him a hug and he hugged her right back, more tightly than he meant to. She came in for a big kiss on his cheek.

The doorbell rang. Trace pulled himself free, grinning at Auntie Lea. Thirty-five hundred potatoes weren't going to peel themselves.

## Acknowledgments

Several years ago, I came across two stories that lodged in my mind and slowly began to merge. I'd read online that the New York Public Library on Fifth Avenue had been built atop the ashes of the Colored Orphan Asylum, which was burned down during the 1863 Draft Riots. Not true. But if you've ever visited the shadowy stacks below that Fifth Avenue landmark, it would be easy to believe that ghosts wander among its shelves of exiled books.

Then I heard the story, and even watched a video on YouTube, of the miraculous rescue of a man whose car had sunk in a lake. With the windows rolled up and the car's electrical system disabled, he tried desperately to break the glass. As water filled the car, arms reached through a window and pulled him to safety. Surfacing, he was lifted onto a raft by emergency workers who had raced to the scene. But when the car was dragged out of the lake, the windows were still tightly rolled up.

Reality is a slippery thing. What principle of science

explains how a person passes through a glass window without breaking it? What version of the facts could justify burning down an orphanage full of children? That fuzzy intersection between fact and fiction seems like the perfect place for a tale to begin.

Many people helped this story take shape, some with advice, some with information, some who may not realize how much I appreciate their input.

Thank you to Sheila Hamanaka, Jackie Carter, and Lisa Holton, coconspirators in storytelling, plot thickening, and brownie consumption, and invaluable sources of inspiration. Thanks to my earliest readers: Rubin Pfeffer for his insightful encouragement; Barbara Lalicki for such kind, constructive feedback; and Lerato Moeti Cummings for the brutal thirteen-year-old frankness I needed to hear. I'm ever thankful to Walter Dean Myers, a master of story structure, and Ellen Hopkins, whose trust that characters will guide the narrative was eye-opening and so true. A huge thanks also to Ginee Seo and Alvina Ling for taking the time to offer insights both generous and wise.

Betsy Bird was incredibly helpful, not only giving me a tour of the stacks below the New York Public Library but also sending me evidence that the Asylum had actually been located a couple of blocks to the north. Facts notwithstanding, I thought a ghost would surely drift a few blocks downtown rather than haunt the nondescript corner of Forty-Fourth Street. Thanks also to Faith Mitchell, who sent along research into the one fatality of that awful event: a young girl killed by the angry mob. I also appreciate how Dwight Johnson, Cynthia Augustine, and Laurent Linn swung into action to help track down information. And thanks also to Taylor Abatiell, who turned my scribbles into a readable version of Trace's family tree.

Chapter by chapter, the lovely ladies of OWW, Our Writers Workshop, helped the story take shape; I'm deeply grateful to Diane Dillon, Donna Grant, Susan Straub, and Fathye Weaver. Their thoughtful feedback, imaginative insights, constant encouragement, and lively company are reflected on every page.

It really does take a village. And an agent. I thank my friend Jerdine Nolen for leading me to Marietta Zacker. Marietta's warmth, true passion for storytelling, and clarity about the market made her the perfect fit. I must credit her for *Trace* becoming more than a file trapped in my computer.

It was my good fortune that the story I had lived

with, wrestled with, and wrangled onto the page landed in the gentle but deft hands of my editor, Rosemary Brosnan. With spot-on instincts, good humor, and profound sensitivity, she made the editing process not only enlightening but surprisingly enjoyable. Somehow, she managed to treat *Trace* like an only child.

Thanks also to her eagle-eyed team: Courtney Stevenson, Emily Rader, and Megan Gendell, who caught all the glitches and asked all the right questions with consummate diplomacy. A mighty thanks to the talented Erin Fitzsimmons and David Curtis for their elegant design of the book. And for the magical, evocative cover, I am indebted to Erwin Madrid, whose work truly captures that intersection between reality and fantasy. The image gave me a delicious chill.

Finally, a special thanks to Linda, Barbara, Art, Keija, and Kali, who know they've been fodder for my stories yet have never once taken legal action. I am endlessly grateful for my mom and dad, Christine and Art Cummings. They convinced us we could fly but kept a net handy. And of course, always, thanks to Chuku Lee, for just about everything.